City of Names

City of Names

by Kevin Brockmeier

Viking

VIKING
Published by the Penguin Group
Penguin Putnam Books for Young Readers,
345 Hudson Street, New York, New York 10014, U.S.A.
Penguin Books Ltd, 80 Strand, London WC2R 0RL, England
Penguin Books Australia Ltd, Ringwood, Victoria, Australia
Penguin Books Canada Ltd, 10 Alcorn Avenue, Toronto, Ontario, Canada M4V 3B2
Penguin Books (N.Z.) Ltd, 182-190 Wairau Road, Auckland 10, New Zealand

Penguin Books Ltd, Registered Offices: Harmondsworth, Middlesex, England

Published in 2002 by Viking, a division of Penguin Putnam Books for Young Readers.

1 3 5 7 9 10 8 6 4 2

Copyright © Kevin Brockmeier, 2002
All rights reserved

LIBRARY OF CONGRESS CATALOGING-IN-PUBLICATION DATA
Brockmeier, Kevin.
City of names / by Kevin Brockmeier.
p. cm.
Summary: After receiving a strange book at school, ten-year-old
Howie Quackenbush discovers that he can transport himself to various
places around his town and he learns something vitally important
about his soon-to-be-born baby sister.
ISBN 0-670-03565-3
[1. Space and time—Fiction. 2. Names, Personal—Fiction.
3. Babies—Fiction.] I. Title
PZ7.B7828 Ci 2002   (Fic)—dc21 2001055910

Printed in U.S.A.
Set in Esprit
Designed by Kelley McIntyre

*For the children at
Lord of Life Learning Center, 1993–1995,
and for Lewis Krain, Sylvia Amsler,
and Margie McGee*

Chapter ①

Before I received the *Secret Guide to North Mellwood* in the mail and met my unborn little sister, my life was pretty normal. I read comic books, I went to school, I played with my friends—that's about it. In fact, the most interesting thing that ever happened to me before the story I'm about to tell you took place, was when I rescued a group of baby birds from my cat, Rhubarb. Rhubarb is a lazy red thing with a loud, rumbling purr. She is roughly the size of a bed pillow, and it is a struggle for her to do even the simplest things, like climb into or out of a chair. My dad says it's hormonal. Anyway, I was outside playing, and I saw that Rhubarb had somehow managed to hoist herself into the tree at the side of our house. She was creeping along a low branch, her fat sagging around the wood like two loaves of bread, and an angry-looking bird was swooping back and forth. I can't tell you what kind of bird she was—I don't know that sort of thing—but if you want to look it up, she had a yellow belly and a blue back and black circles around her eyes. It turned out that Rhubarb was dragging herself toward a nest. There were three fuzzy little heads peeking out from it. I pulled Rhubarb off the branch and brought her back inside.

After I shut her in my bedroom, I went to the sink to wash the dishes. Rhubarb had left a few deep scratches in my arm, and they stung when they hit the soapy water. The bird that had been flying around the tree landed on the windowsill above the sink. She didn't look angry anymore. In fact, she looked positively cheerful, so cheerful that she began to whistle a song. She stood there whistling until I finished every last dish in the sink.

So I saved three baby birds from my cat Rhubarb, and their mother thanked me with a serenade. That's it—the most interesting thing that had ever happened to me.

What else? When the story I'm about to tell you began, my mom was pregnant. My dad and I had been watching a TV show called *Freak Accidents: When Bearded Ladies Attack* when she found out about it. She came into the living room waving a little blue baton and screaming, "It's a cross! It's a cross!" The bearded ladies had us both so spooked that we jumped in our chairs. We could see that Mom was excited about something, but we didn't know what. "Across what?" my dad said. "Across where?"

It turns out that the baton my mom was waving around was a pregnancy-test stick. I don't know all the details, but apparently you pee on the stick, and if a cross appears you're going to have a baby. My mom was going to have a baby.

That was five months ago, and now it was nothing but babies at our house. Babies and babies and babies. My parents bought a crib and a playpen and began turning my dad's study into a nursery. They decorated the walls with this yellow wallpaper that had pictures of chicks and bunnies around the border. They stocked the hall closet with diapers and bottles and pacifiers. The baby hadn't even been born yet, and already it was filling the house. I wasn't sure how I felt about all this; after all, *I* had never decided to have a baby, but it looked like I was going to be a big brother one way or the other. Would I even *like* the baby? I wondered. Would it like me? What would happen if the baby bit me, or if I accidentally sat on it? I worried about this sort of thing. When I forgot to do my chores or tracked mud across the carpet, my parents had conversations with me that started, "You know, your little brother or sister is going to look up to you very much," and ended, "so you need to do such and such." But I had no idea how to be a big brother. That's what I kept thinking.

We didn't know yet whether the baby was going to be a boy or a girl. There is a camera the doctors can use to look inside the mother's stomach and answer questions like that, but my parents wanted everything to be a surprise. They talked a lot about what they were going to

3

name the baby, suggesting boy names and girl names to each other, but their discussions never lasted more than thirty seconds. The reason for this is that my mom took the discussions very seriously—her face would brighten up, and she would make these big, sweeping gestures with her hands—but my dad could never resist suggesting funny names to bug her. A typical breakfast conversation would go something like this:

MOM: (*spooning sugar onto her cereal*) What do you think about Daisy if it's a girl? Daisy! Isn't that a lovely name? (*singing*) "Daisy, Daisy, give me your answer, do—"

DAD: (*stirring his coffee*) Daisy is a fine name. But have you thought about any other flower names?

MOM: Oh, I have—but Rose is too common, and I don't care for Lily or Iris.

DAD: How about Sweet Pea?

MOM: (*grimacing*) Sweet Pea? Oh, a joke. Ha, ha. Very funny, Lewis.

DAD: (*trying hard not to laugh*) Not Sweet Pea? Well, then, how about Geranium? Or Ragwort? How about Wax Plant? (*singing*) "Wax Plant, Wax Plant, give me your answer do—"

MOM: That's enough.

DAD: (*smiling*) Horehound? (*beaming*) Rhododendron? (*guffawing with laughter*) Venus Flytrap?

It was at this point that my mom would usually send a

spoonful of cereal flying through the air, and corn flakes and sugar would come sprinkling down over my father like snow.

Names are important. This is particularly true when you're a kid. My best friend, for instance, is named Kevin Bugg. With a last name like Bugg, he was bound to get picked on at school, and he does, but at least his parents had the good sense to call him Kevin. Imagine if they had chosen a name like Harold. My best friend Kevin Bugg is a chubby kid and kind of a slob (he's my best friend, but he is). He also gets the chills pretty easily, and for most of the year he wears this huge down coat with a puffy hood that makes him look even bigger than he really is. He wears this coat even indoors.

If his parents had named him Harold, I feel certain the kids at school would call him Big Harry Bugg.

Some of the other kids in my class are Sam Purcell, Lucy Horn, Susan Goins, Lionel Beef, Nathaniel Hawthorne, Melissa McGee, Ha Nguyen (it's pronounced Win), Michael Jenkins, Casey Goss (who's a boy), and Casey Robinson (who's a girl).

I am ten years old and in the fifth grade at Larry Boone Elementary School. According to Michael Jenkins, who's kind of a know-it-all, Larry Boone was a famous Revolutionary War hero, but I've looked him up in the encyclopedia, and I can't find any mention of him there. Maybe he was actually a famous inventor or a football star or some kind of evil genius. Or maybe he was just some nobody they named a school after. It's the sort of thing I wonder about. There's a bronze statue of Larry Boone in the school courtyard, and in the statue he is wearing blue jeans and a sweater vest. Did Revolutionary War heroes wear blue jeans and sweater vests? I don't think so.

School is okay most of the time. I have a few really close friends, people like Kevin Bugg and Casey Robinson, which is nice. Also, I can always make everybody laugh during Question and Answer Time, even the teacher. It's a gift I have. I'm good at English and science and health and long division. In fact, I get A's and B's in almost everything—everything but penmanship. In penmanship I get D's and D+'s. My teachers write notes on my report card that say things like, "Your son Howie is a smart boy, but he writes like he's a barnyard animal." That's my name, by the way, Howie.

Howie Quackenbush, actually.

I get picked on.

Chapter 2

Every night I go to sleep happy. My bed is warm, my blankets are soft, and my cat is making snoozing noises on the floor, wheezy little sighs that she gives through her nose. The moon makes my curtains glow with a yellow light, and all my stuff is piled in heaps around the room. There are stacks of comic books beside my desk. There are footballs and hockey sticks and superhero action figures. There's a city on wheels that my Aunt Margie made me for Christmas last year: the city is built on top of a wagon, and the buildings inside are on steel tracks so that they roll around and shift places whenever you pull it. My Aunt Margie creates neat wooden sculptures like this that she paints herself and gives to all her nieces and nephews on Christmases and birthdays. Lately I've been collecting a kind of toy called Egg-Bots. Egg-

Bots are these heavy plastic eggs that unfold to turn into robots, and the robots can be folded around on themselves again to turn into robot chickens. They sound sort of stupid, I guess, but they're actually really cool. The eggs don't look like regular eggs—they're colored gold and black and silver, and they have these grooves and ridges on them that make them look sort of scientific. Anyway, as I was saying, every night I go to sleep happy, and every morning I wake up with dry boogers in the corner of my eyes.

I don't know why this should be. I asked my mom and dad once how the boogers got there, whether they formed there naturally or whether they simply traveled up from my nose somehow, but they couldn't answer me. I even asked my teacher once. My teacher's name is Miss Hufnagel, but she is not as scary as she sounds. Every day following afternoon recess we have something Miss Hufnagel calls Question and Answer Time. During Question and Answer Time, we are supposed to ask Miss Hufnagel any questions we have about the school-work we have been doing. Then, if there is time, we can ask her about other things—about current events or how things work or upcoming tests or just about anything.

One day, near the end of Question and Answer Time, I asked Miss Hufnagel about the boogers in my eyes. "Miss Hufnagel?" I said, raising my hand.

"What is it, Howie?"

"How come when I wake up in the morning, there are boogers in my eyes?"

The other kids immediately started to howl. Melissa McGee rolled her eyes, and Kevin Bugg turned around in his seat and grinned at me.

Miss Hufnagel's chin kept twitching into new shapes, and I could see that she was trying not to laugh. She pressed her lips together into a thin white line. Eventually she said, "I'll booger you," but she never did answer my question.

Sorry I've talked for so long about boogers. It was sort of an accident.

Most days, after Question and Answer Time, we have our social studies lesson, the last lesson of the day, where we learn about people from other cultures—people like Bogana and Wana, two Ethiopian kids who go to school in a hut made out of clay, or Sam and Marie, Native Americans who live on a reservation with their parents. But about once a month, the mailman will deliver a large cardboard box to our classroom, a box with bright red tape around the seams and the creaking sound of Styrofoam peanuts inside, and Miss Hufnagel will hand out the books we have ordered.

That's really where this story begins, with the books. Every class at Larry Boone Elementary School receives *The Kids' Club Book Service Newsletter* on the first Monday of each month, and the books themselves come about three weeks later. *The Kids' Club Book Service Newsletter* is a four-page catalog of books for children and what they call "young adults" (which you would think means people like my Uncle Billy, who is twenty-two years old and about to finish college, but which actually just means smart kids). They have picture books, novels, maze and puzzle books, choose-your-own-adventure stories, dictionaries, science books—you name it. If you want to buy any of the books from the newsletter, you have to return the order form to class on Friday, along with a check from your parents. Everybody wants to order books from the newsletter, even the kids who don't like to read. Most of us order three or four if we can convince our parents to pay for them. It's no good being the only person in the room who doesn't get to crowd around the teacher's desk when the mailman arrives with that big brown box. It would be like not getting a gift at a Christmas party—which believe me, feels rotten. I know, because it happened to me once. When I was in the second grade, our class had a Christmas gift exchange. Two weeks before the Christmas party, we picked names from a hat on little rectangles of paper. I drew Casey Robinson's name and bought her a Nerf football (which was what she told me she wanted) and a box of chocolates (which my mom and dad said was a much sweeter present for a little girl). Ben Hoover drew my name and bought me a wristwatch that could squirt real water, but on the way to school our bus driver caught him squirting Susan Goins and took it away from him. The bus driver never did give it back, and he even uses it sometimes to squirt kids who are standing in their seats. It makes me mad every time I see that watch.

It was a cold, wet day in January when the mailman delivered our shipment of books. Our mailman's name is Mr. Haddadi, and he always smiles at us before he leaves, saying, "Many blessings to you, precious little children," which is exactly what he did that afternoon. A blanket of snow had lain over the city of North Mellwood for almost two weeks, but outside it was raining, and I could see from the window that all but a few gray clumps of the snow had melted away into the grass. Somehow the sight of all that rain washing through the street made me feel much colder than the snow ever had, and for a moment I wished I was my best friend Kevin Bugg, in his heavy down jacket with the puffy hood. After we finished Question and Answer Time, Miss Hufnagel lifted the box of books onto her desk, and an excited murmur went up from the class. First she opened the box with a pair of scissors, sliding one of the blades along the seams of red tape at the top. Then she removed the order slip and the Styrofoam peanuts. Next she began sorting the books into twenty separate stacks, one for each student in the class. And finally she called us all to gather around her desk.

Nina Fitzsimmons stood beside me trying to work a ring over the knuckle of her little finger. "I ordered *The A-maze-ing Book of Mazes*, *A Little Princess*, and *Horace Goes Hog Wild*," she said. "What did you order?"

"I ordered *Charlie and the Chocolate Factory*, *Tales of the Presidents*, and *101 Pickle Jokes*," I told her.

"*101 Pickle Jokes*!?" she said. "I remember reading

11

the newsletter and thinking, 'Who in their right mind would possibly order *101 Pickle Jokes?*'"

I didn't know what to say to that, so I just shrugged my shoulders. "Pickles aren't so bad," I muttered.

Miss Hufnagel called our names one by one, in alphabetical order. Since my name is Quackenbush, I'm always near the bottom of the list when it comes to alphabetical order. In fact, the only students in my class whose names come after mine are Casey Robinson and Jim Zug. This is a good thing during spelling bees and math contests, but a bad thing when teachers are handing out books. By the time Miss Hufnagel reached my name the afternoon bell had already sounded, and I had to shove my books straight into my backpack and run outside to catch the bus. I sprinted past a big kid in a green army jacket who was pushing a little kid with a blue umbrella against the wall. I'm always afraid that the bus will leave without me and I will have to walk all the way through town and across Mellwood Reservoir to get back home, though this has never once happened to anyone at my school. Casey Robinson followed behind me, and we took the last two seats on the bus, both right up front. Jim Zug's grandmother picks him up in the afternoon, so he doesn't have to worry about this sort of thing.

It was still raining, and Casey Robinson and I each picked raindrops to race each other with during the bus ride. We coached them across the window until they got too heavy and went puddling down to the bottom of the glass. I was too busy, and too wet, to look at my books, so it wasn't until I got home that I realized a mistake had been made. Instead of *Charlie and the Chocolate Factory, Tales of the Presidents,* and *101 Pickle Jokes,* I had been given *Charlie and the Chocolate Factory, Tales of the Presidents,* and something else entirely.

Chapter 3

My cat Rhubarb was sleeping on top of the television, slumped over the cable box. I find her there almost every afternoon—she likes it because it's warm, I guess. Actually, it would be more accurate to say that Rhubarb was sleeping *surrounding* the cable box, since she covered every single inch of it and spilled over a bit onto the television. If I hadn't already known that the cable box was underneath her, I would never have guessed it was there at all.

I poured some cat food into Rhubarb's food dish, got a soda for myself out of the refrigerator, and went upstairs to my bedroom, where I opened the soda and emptied it into a glass. I like to drink my soda from a glass because of what I call the Fizz Effect. If you put your nose to a glass of soda immediately after it has been poured, you will get this cool tingly sensation in your head that makes you feel like you have just bitten into a really strong mint. Try it.

After I had finished my soda, I settled down on the floor to look at the books I had ordered—*Charlie and the Chocolate Factory*, *Tales of the Presidents*, and . . . The third book I found in my backpack was not *101 Pickle Jokes*. It was not anything from *The Kids' Club Book Service Newsletter* at all. It was something called the *Secret Guide to North Mellwood*, and on the cover it showed a photograph of my town that must have been taken from an airplane. I could see Larry Boone Elementary School and the Mellwood Reservoir and the Doughnut Brothers doughnut factory. I could see the swimming pool where I swam in the summer, covered for the winter with a sheet of green plastic. I could even see my own house in the center of our block, with two big trees in the front yard and one small tree on the side. I sorted through the pencils and notebooks in my backpack looking for *101 Pickle Jokes*, but it wasn't there. What, I wondered, was the *Secret Guide to North Mellwood*? And where on earth was *101 Pickle Jokes*?

I flipped open to the middle section of the *Secret Guide to North Mellwood* to see what I would find. It was as much a map, it seemed, as it was a book. All of the pages except the first two opened into a single large sheet of paper, which I unfolded. It covered almost half of the open space on my bedroom floor and was about as large as the spotted mat they use in Twister, if you've ever played that game. The picture on the map was identical to the picture on the book's cover, except much larger. I could see all of the same things there that I could on the cover—all the houses and streets and buildings and trees—except in much greater detail. I noticed that on top of each building was a small white space with a word printed on the inside. On top of my house, for instance, there was the word GUDDLE. I closed the map and read the paragraph on the first page of the book.

Welcome, consumer! You have made a wise choice in your purchase of the Secret Guide to North Mellwood. *Many hours of fun and excitement await you. The* Secret Guide to North Mellwood *is easy to use. Most people don't realize that every place in North Mellwood has two names—a false name and a true name. For instance, the hamburger stand in the Mellwood Mall is known as Lucky's Burger Hut— this is its false name. Its true name is* LEBERWURST. *The enclosed map will provide the true name of every location in North Mellwood. You will find that know- ing the true name of a place has many advantages. It will help you to better understand that place's inner nature. It will improve your hand-eye coordination. And it will make for fast and efficient travel. To visit any of the places in the* Secret Guide to North Mellwood, *you may go to one of the five portals shown on the reverse side of this page. Simply knock three times on the portal and then recite the true name of the place you wish to visit. When you have*

16

completed your visit, recite the true name once again and you will be returned to the portal from which you started. The makers of the Secret Guide to North Mellwood *are not liable for any injuries or misfortunes that may result from the use of this book. Such injuries and misfortunes may include but are not limited to nausea, dry mouth, indigestion, forgetfulness, runny nose, reduced sense of smell, bankruptcy, loss of friends, loss of appetite, inability to sneeze, dismemberment, transformation into giant bug, headaches, death, inability to play the piano (or other musical instrument), and inexplicable sudden aging. Good luck and happy traveling!*

I turned the page to take a look at the five portals the author had mentioned. Most of them I didn't recognize— there were a couple of warehouses, what appeared to be a blank wall in somebody's house, and a hollowed-out tree beside a bunch of other trees. The tree seemed vaguely familiar, but this was probably just because it looked like every other hollowed-out tree I've ever seen in my life. One of the portals, though, was an image I knew as well as my own face: it was the bronze statue of Larry Boone in front of my elementary school. How lucky that the portal was so conveniently located! I decided that I would test the *Secret Guide to North Mellwood* the next day after school to see if it worked. I doubted that it would (I mean, whoever heard of magic portals?), but you never know about things like that. I would have to invite Kevin Bugg to test it with me, but otherwise I wanted to keep the book a secret.

Just as I was putting the book back in my backpack, I heard my parents coming in downstairs. "Howie!" my dad called. "Time for dinner!" I washed my hands and went down to the kitchen. I could smell Mexican food, and I knew that my parents had picked up dinner from Señor Taco. Lately we had been eating food from Señor Taco as often as three times a week. My mom was always getting cravings for their chicken and avocado burritos. Before that it was potato sticks, and before that, black licorice. I asked Mom once what it felt like to crave something when you were pregnant. Did it mean that you just felt like eating something, or was there more to it than that? She told me, "I don't know what it's like for other women, but for me it means that I can taste a certain food all the time. If I have a craving for potato sticks, then I will actually taste potato sticks in my mouth. The only way to get rid of the taste is to go out and eat some potato sticks. When I was pregnant with you, I wanted nothing but coconut chews and coleslaw." I hate coconut chews, and I hate coleslaw, and I always have. I wondered if this was because my mother had eaten too much of them when I was in her stomach.

As we were eating dinner, my dad asked me how my day had been. "Pretty good," I said. "We had to stay inside during recess because it was raining."

"Did anything interesting happen?" he asked.

"No," I lied. "Not really."

18

My mom was paging through a book she had bought called *3,500 Names for Baby*. "What about Franklin for a boy?" she interrupted us. "It means 'a free man.' I like that."

My dad answered, "But I had my heart set on Dig Dug, honey."

Dig Dug was the name of a popular video game at Star Systems Video Parlor, a sort of teen hangout full of arcade games and Skee-Ball lanes and novelty machines. Star Systems was owned by Mr. Bugg, my best friend Kevin Bugg's father.

"We're *not* naming our baby Dig Dug," my mom said.

"And why not? Dig Dug is a perfectly good name. Any child would be *proud* to be named Dig Dug Quackenbush," my dad said with a flourish.

"Dig Dug is a silly name, and I don't know why you can't take this seriously."

"Okay, okay," said my dad. "We'll compromise. We'll name the baby Digby Douglas. Digby is a normal name, and Douglas is a normal name, and that way we can call him Dig Dug for short."

My mom was squeezing her burrito so hard that little wedges of chicken were falling out onto the table, and I decided that this would be as good a time as any to ask my question. "Speaking of names," I said, "do either of you have any idea what the word 'guddle' means?"

"No idea," said my mom.

"Never heard of it," said my dad. "Guddle . . ." He thought for a moment. "Are you sure that it's a real word?"

19

My dad has a set of heavy, expensive dictionaries that fill an entire bookshelf in our living room. They are called the *Oxford English Dictionary*. The list of words in the *Oxford English Dictionary* is so long that many of the letters take up more than one volume—there are four separate *M* books, just to give you an idea, and the definition for the word "the" goes on for three whole pages.

That night, before I went to bed, I looked up the word "guddle" in the second *G* volume of the *Oxford English Dictionary*.

It means "to catch a fish by groping in the water."

Chapter ④

I was still curious to see what had happened to my copy of *101 Pickle Jokes*, so when I got to school the next day, I asked Miss Hufnagel if she had found any extra books in the box. "Not a one," she said. "But I do have some Styrofoam peanuts left over. Are you missing a book, Howie?"

"No, ma'am," I said. "I was just curious."

It was not raining that day, so we had recess outside. We wobbled down the hall in our big winter coats and hit the playground at a run. Ordinarily, I play goalie on one of the soccer teams, but I wanted to see whether anyone else had gotten my copy of *101 Pickle Jokes* by mistake. I also wanted to see whether anyone had ever heard of the *Secret Guide to North Mellwood*. I couldn't come right out and ask them about it, though, so I came up with a few questions that I thought might help me sniff out the truth. I felt like a detective. "Did you order *101 Pickle Jokes* from *The Kids' Club Book Service Newsletter*? No? Did you happen to receive a copy of *101 Pickle Jokes* by mistake? No? Did you notice anything strange about the books you *did* receive yesterday?" No one had.

Nathaniel Hawthorne, who was tagging along, said to me, "Why are you asking everyone the same questions over and over again?"

"I'll tell you later," I said, and continued my search.

During our math lesson, I passed a note to Kevin Bugg. Whenever Miss Hufnagel caught us passing notes, she would collect them and read them to the class, so I watched carefully as the note made its way from desk to desk. Kevin Bugg is easily startled and often jumps in his chair when people tap him on the shoulder, so passing notes to him is particularly dangerous. Fortunately, Miss Hufnagel was writing a math problem on the board when my note reached his desk. "Urgent!" the note read. "Meet me after school today by the statue of Larry Boone. I might have something interesting to show you. Don't tell anyone!"

"So what's up?" Kevin Bugg asked when we met by the statue. A mass of white clouds had been gathering in the sky all afternoon, and it looked like it was going to snow again. In fact, I could see a few tiny, dry-looking flakes falling from the clouds as we stood there, spinning around in the wind and then melting as soon as they hit the ground. A bunch of kids ran past us to the bus. A big kid in a green army jacket walked by carrying a blue umbrella.

I waited until nobody was watching and then pulled Kevin Bugg around to the back side of the statue, away from all the cars and buses. "Okay," I said. "Here goes." I removed the *Secret Guide to North Mellwood* from my backpack.

"What's that?" Kevin Bugg asked.

"It's a book I got yesterday. I'll tell you all about it in just a minute. But first what I need you to do is watch and let me know what happens, okay?"

"What about the bus?" said Kevin Bugg. "You know we're going to miss the bus."

"If this works," I told him, "we won't have to worry about the bus. And if it doesn't, it will only take a second for us to find out."

I unfolded a few squares of the map to make sure that the true name of my home had not changed since last night. It was still the same: GUDDLE. "All right," I said to Kevin Bugg. "Get ready to tell me what happens." The instructions did not say exactly where you were supposed to knock on Larry Boone in order to open the portal, so I knocked three times on the space behind his left knee. It made a sort of hollow clunking sound— *clunk, clunk, clunk.* I stood back and waited for the portal to open.

Nothing happened. I was expecting to see a door swing open, or a gate filled with brilliant green light. But instead the statue just stood there. What a rip-off.

23

"Is that it?" said Kevin Bugg. "Can we catch the bus now?"

"Wait a minute. I might as well finish," I said. I pressed my palm to the statue and screwed my eyes shut, and though I fully expected to be left standing right there by Kevin Bugg, I went ahead and whispered my house's true name. "Guddle," I said.

Before I even opened my eyes, I could tell that something had changed. The difference between the inside and the outside is unmistakable. Even if you have your eyes shut, even if the day is as still as a hall closet, there is a sort of energy to the outside that the inside doesn't have. It has to do with the air, and the weather, and all the living things that are there. If you've ever suddenly found yourself inside when you thought you were outside, or outside when you thought you were inside, you will know what I'm talking about. I could no longer feel the wind blowing on my skin. A clock was ticking behind me. When I moved my hand, it bumped into something soft. "*Prrp?*" went the something soft, and I opened my eyes.

I was standing in my own living room. Rhubarb was looking up at me from on top of the cable box, but she didn't seem at all surprised to see me. I was so excited that I gave a shout. "Yes! It worked!" I said, and Rhubarb made a funny sniffing noise and closed her eyes.

I didn't want to keep Kevin Bugg waiting, so I said "guddle" again and immediately found myself standing outside my school by the statue of Larry Boone. Kevin Bugg was groping around in the air, saying, "Hello? Hello?

Hello?" and trying to figure out where I had gone. "Holy smokes!" he said when I reappeared. He was the only person I knew who ever said this—*holy smokes*—and he said it all the time. "What happened to you?"

"What did it look like?" I said. "What did you see?"

"First you were here, and then all of a sudden you weren't. And it smelled terrible."

"What do you mean it smelled terrible?"

"It smelled like rotten eggs," he said. He sniffed the air. "Well, it's gone now. But it was here a minute ago."

I told Kevin Bugg all about the *Secret Guide to North Mellwood*—about the map and the portals, the true names and the set of instructions. He believed me right away. This kind of surprised me, but I suppose if you've seen a person disappear into thin air, you'll be willing to believe almost anything. "I want to try it," he said.

"I don't know," I said. The idea of Kevin Bugg hopping all over town through the portal made me feel a little bit selfish. It was my *Secret Guide*, after all, and I'd barely even used it myself. "Didn't you read the warning list in the instructions? What if you get sick or start forgetting things or transform into a giant bug?"

"I'm already a giant bug," said Kevin Bugg.

I laughed. "Good point," I said. "Well, maybe we can try it together. But you have to promise not to tell anyone else about it."

"Perfect," he answered. "I want to go to my house first, and then we can go wherever you want."

We waited until all of the buses had pulled away, and

then waited some more until most of the teachers' cars had left. Then we found Kevin Bugg's house on the map. Its true name was KITTLE-PINS, which I later learned is a game kind of like bowling, played with a ball that you swing from a rope. We both knocked three times on the statue of Larry Boone, and then, in the same breath, we both said "kittle-pins." I thought it was important that we say "kittle-pins" at the same time because I didn't know exactly how the portal worked. I was afraid that we might get separated.

"One, two, three—kittle-pins!" We were standing in Kevin Bugg's driveway. It was a good thing that we landed outside, since Kevin Bugg's mom works at home, and if we had suddenly appeared right in front of her, there's no telling what she would have done. She has a heart condition, and we might really have scared her. At the very least, she would have called my parents, and I didn't really want to tell them about the *Secret Guide to North Mellwood*. "It worked!" said Kevin Bugg. "It really worked!"

"Of course it worked," I said. I felt like an old pro, even though I had only transported once before. "And here's how we get back to the statue. One, two, three—kittle-pins!"

We spent the next hour or so leaping from place to place through the portal. It took us a while, but eventually we discovered most of its tricks. At first I was a little bit worried that we might say one of the true names by accident and end up at the bottom of a lake or in the middle of a girls' bathroom somewhere, but the true names were all so crazy that there was no real danger of that happening. The true name of Star Systems Video Parlor, for instance, was HURDY-GURDY. The true name of my Aunt Margie's house was SHIBUI. The true name of the entrance to the Mellwood Mall was FLOCCINAUCINI-HILIPILIFICATION (which is also a real word, believe it or not, and means "the act of estimating something as worthless").

We discovered that when we knocked on Larry Boone and said a true name, we would always appear in exactly the same place—when we said the true name of my house, for instance, we would always land right in my living room, directly next to the television, and never anywhere else. In order to transport back, we had to repeat the true name again from roughly that same spot. If we were too far away from where we had landed, the portal just wouldn't work. Also, Kevin Bugg and I didn't have to say the true name at exactly the same moment in order to be transported from the statue together. In fact, as long as the one who knocked on the statue said the true name, and the other one held on to him, we would both be sent through the portal together. We didn't have to knock in the hollow of Larry Boone's knee, either—we could have knocked on his foot, for instance, or on his hip, or on his forehead if we could have reached that high. But the hollow of his knee was as good a place as any, and since that's where we knocked the first time, and it was mostly hidden from view, that's the spot we usually chose.

We said "tomium" and transported to Reservoir Park. We said "pogonotomy" and transported to the K Street Barber Shop. We said "alimentary" and transported to the Super Crazy Prices Convenience Store, where we bought blueberry slush drinks and ranch-flavored potato chips. Twice we saw the other kids in our class riding by on the school bus. The first time we were hanging around outside Star Systems Video Parlor. The bus rounded the corner and was just suddenly *there*, and we panicked and said "hurdy-gurdy" again as it drove past. I could see Casey Robinson waving to us from the front window as we vanished from sight. A few minutes later, we were sitting on the stoop outside Kevin Bugg's grandmother's house, six or seven blocks away, when the bus passed us again. This time we didn't vanish. We just lay back on the stoop and waved. Some of the other kids saw us and waved back, but Casey Robinson just sat staring through the window. Her face looked pale and sick, as if someone had punched her in the stomach. I guess we weren't being very careful.

Every time we used the portal, a small odor of rotten eggs would rise into the air around us. We smelled it by the statue, and we smelled it in my living room, and we smelled it outside the video parlor, but it always vanished after a second or two.

It was almost time for dinner when Kevin Bugg and I decided to call it quits for the day. We agreed that we would use the portal to get to school tomorrow instead of riding the bus, if we could. I would simply have to remember not to say "guddle" that night, and Kevin Bugg would have to remember not to say "kittle-pins." We knocked three times on the statue, and then we transported home.

I noticed that the smell of rotten eggs was peculiarly strong as we left. The odor seemed to increase with each use of the portal, and the bigger it got, I guessed, the more it would linger.

Chapter 5

I have sort of a crush on Casey Robinson. I've had sort of a crush on Casey Robinson ever since I was six years old, on my very first day at Larry Boone Elementary School. Most people seem to think that boys my age don't like girls. We're supposed to pull their hair and throw dirt at them, and they're supposed to call us names and run away from us. And then there's the whole cootie thing. I don't know where people get these ideas. All I can say is that I've liked girls ever since I can remember, and so has every other boy in my class. I met Casey Robinson on the first day of first grade during something called Afternoon Free Time. Afternoon Free Time was something we had only in the first grade—we haven't had it since. It was supposed to help us make the change between kindergarten, which was pretty much *all* free time, and the rest of elementary school, which is pretty much all work. Anyway, a bunch of kids were playing records in the corner of the classroom, and I went over to join them. They asked me what my name was, and I said, "Howie Quackenbush." All of a sudden they were all rolling around laughing on the floor. Casey Robinson was the only one who didn't join in with them. Kids tend to make duck noises the first time they hear my name—it's just what they do—but she didn't do that either. I'll never forget that day.

I've always been sort of proud that her name comes right after my own in alphabetical order. The roll call goes like this: Ha Nguyen, Sam Purcell, Howie Quackenbush, Casey Robinson. It gives me a feeling of satisfaction every time I hear our names together like that. When we were in the third grade, a kid named Jason Reynolds transferred into our class from another school, and his name fell right between ours like a wart. I never did like Jason Reynolds, and I think it was just because of what his name did to mine. In fact, every time I saw him, I got mad—I know that sounds crazy, but I did. Fortunately, Jason Reynolds was not very smart and got sent back to the second grade after only two weeks.

Casey Robinson wears her hair in a long, red-brown tassel that sways across her back when she runs. She is taller than me. She has a nice friendly smile that she uses just often enough that you don't get used to seeing it on her; it's a little bit tight at the corners, as if somebody had placed a single stitch on either side of her mouth, but it's still a good smile. Every so often I will see her in the grocery store or at the movie theater—someplace outside of school where I'm not expecting to bump into her—and without fail, the first thing she does is give me that smile, like she hasn't seen me in weeks. Whenever that happens, my stomach gives a standing leap.

Sometimes I think that Casey Robinson likes me. I mean, I know that she *likes* me, but I think that maybe she *likes me* likes me. We do sit together on the bus every day, and it's a fact that she never makes fun of my name. Even Kevin Bugg makes fun of my name sometimes. I wonder what it would be like to kiss her. Someday, when I'm feeling brave, I'm going to try it.

That very night, after Kevin Bugg and I were finished using the portal, Casey Robinson called me at home. She had never called me at home before—in fact, no girl had ever called me at home before. I was surprised when the telephone rang and my mom yelled, "It's for you, Howie. It's a girl."

I don't have my own telephone, so I had to run downstairs and take the call in the kitchen. My parents were watching me from the living room with big grins on their faces. "Hello?" I said.

"Howie? This is Casey." She sounded nervous. "I'm just calling to see if you're all right."

"I'm okay," I said. "Uh, how are you?"

"I'm a little bit worried. You didn't take the bus home after school. And then I thought I saw you with Kevin Bugg, but now I'm not so sure I did. Is there something going on?" she asked.

I felt bad that I had scared her, but I couldn't tell her about the *Secret Guide to North Mellwood*, at least not right then. My parents were listening in from the living room. "There is," I said, "but I can't talk about it tonight. I promise I'll tell you, though. I'll tell you sometime soon."

"Are you sure you're okay?" she asked.

"I'm fine," I said. "But I've gotta go."

"Okay," said Casey Robinson. "See you tomorrow. Good night, Howie."

A little shiver went through my shoulders when she said my name.

The next morning, I tried to use the portal to return to school, but I couldn't get it to work. Kevin Bugg was waiting for me on the bus, and he said that he couldn't get it to work, either. The effect of the true names must have worn off overnight. I wasn't sure exactly how long the effect lasted, but I knew now that it wouldn't last forever. This was useful information.

Casey Robinson asked me during lunch that day if I was ready to tell her what was going on yet. Actually, she didn't ask me—she just raised her eyebrows and gave me this look, but I knew what the look meant. "Not today," I said, placing my hand on my heart. "Monday. I promise. I'll tell you on Monday."

It was Friday, and my mom was picking me up early to take me to get my teeth cleaned. I hate going to the dentist to get my teeth cleaned. I know that everybody hates this, but for me it's particularly painful. The reason is because of my dental hygienist, Miss Joyce. Miss Joyce is about a hundred years old, and her hand shakes in my mouth. She's always poking me in the gums with that little metal spear dental hygienists use to scrape the plaque off your teeth. To top things off, when my tongue moves while she's cleaning my teeth, she grabs it between her fingers and holds it out of the way. Nothing feels more *wrong* than having your tongue grabbed by somebody. My parents and I call Miss Joyce the Dragon Lady. Even if it weren't for her—and I keep hoping that she's going to retire—I would still dislike going to see the dentist. For one thing, the gritty, cherry-flavored toothpaste dentists use to polish your teeth always makes me want to gag. I remember that I used to like the taste of this toothpaste, but now that I'm older I hate it. People say that your tastes change as you grow older, and that must be what happened to me. I like broccoli and green beans now, and I used to hate them. I hate cherry-flavored toothpaste, and I used to love it. Go figure.

I didn't have any cavities that day, so as we left, I got to select a toy from the toy chest by the reception desk. I picked a fortune-telling fish—a slinky little piece of plastic foil shaped to look like a goldfish, which is supposed to tell your fortune by how it changes shape when you hold it in your hand. I placed it delicately in my palm, and it curled together until its tip touched its tail. "A Happy Change," it meant.

Chapter

I didn't use the *Secret Guide to North Mellwood* at all over the weekend. So far I had only used it that one day with Kevin Bugg, and all we had done with it was bounce around from place to place as if it were some sort of magic taxi. I felt like I was just tinkering around with it, and I wanted to put it to better use. The only time I even thought about trying to summon a portal was when I saw a hollowed-out old oak tree on the side of the house down the street. I thought that the tree might be the portal that was pictured inside the *Secret Guide to North Mellwood* alongside the blank wall, the two warehouses, and the statue of Larry Boone. So I knocked on it three times and said "guddle," but the tree was just a tree, and nothing happened.

My parents spent the weekend putting in an intercom system between the nursery, the living room, and their bedroom. The intercom was supposed to alert them if the baby was crying or coughing or complaining, or even if she was just being too quiet ("suspiciously quiet," that's the phrase they kept using). While they were working, they talked about the schools the baby would go to and the clothes the baby would wear. They talked about whether they should stock up on baby food now or wait until they had learned something more about the baby's appetite. They talked again and again about the names they were considering. (My mom's current favorites were "Rowan" for a boy and "Claire" for a girl, and my dad was still leaning toward "Dig Dug.") I was getting tired of the whole thing. Everything was *baby* this and *baby* that, and it seemed like we never talked about anything else. It was wearing me down. I knew that I would probably love the baby when it was born—probably—but just then I needed a break from it for a while.

My parents must have sensed this because they suggested that I eat dinner Saturday night with my Aunt Margie.

My Aunt Margie is my dad's older sister. He also has two younger brothers, but Aunt Margie is the only one who lives in town. Her house is filled with hundreds of painted wood sculptures—marionette puppets, dogs on curved rocking-chair supports, chunky Eskimo figures. She even has an extra kitchen, a fake one, with life-size wooden sculptures of all her kitchen appliances—the refrigerator and the toaster and such. There is actual wooden food in the refrigerator, and the cabinets are all stocked with wooden cans and boxes. Aunt Margie's sculptures fill the whole house, except for one room that she keeps completely empty. She calls this room "the White Room," and she uses it to meditate.

That Saturday night she took me to eat at the Three Monkeys Restaurant, an Asian food place which is right across the street from her house. We both ordered the same dish, the Three Monkeys House Platter. "So you're all babied out, huh?" Aunt Margie said when the food arrived.

I shrugged my shoulders.

"I know the feeling. I was six years old when your father was born, and then your Uncle Billy and your Uncle Edward were both born by the time I was eight. Imagine being the only child in the house your whole life and then—*boom, boom, boom*—three new babies in a row."

"Did you and Dad ever fight when you were little?"

"Oh, all the time," Aunt Margie said. "I mean, we didn't really *fight*. I was so much bigger than your father was. But we argued constantly. Your Uncle Billy and your Uncle Edward fought, and your father and I argued. We used to argue over the silliest things, like who would wear which Halloween costume, or who would get which lollipop when we went to the bank. I was always right, of course." She laughed.

"Tell me about the Halloween costumes," I said. I was eating an extremely spicy portion of chicken and yellow rice, and every few seconds I had to take a gulp of water.

"Well," said Aunt Margie, "your grandmother used to sew our Halloween costumes for us every year. The first time your father was old enough to go trick-or-treating with me, she had two costume patterns to work from, a ghost and a fish. She asked us who wanted to be the ghost and who wanted to be the fish, and we both wanted to be the ghost. We fought for *days* about it. Eventually, your grandmother said she was sick of hearing us argue, and she told us that *she* would decide for herself. Halloween came, and she had sewn two fish costumes. No ghost costumes at all. I guess she wanted to teach us a lesson. There's a picture of the two of us dressed up in the costumes. We have these huge fins sprouting out of our backs, and we're both carrying little jack-o'-lantern candy baskets." She was laughing. "The frowns on our faces! Our dad—your grandfather—is standing behind us with this big grin, and Lewis and I look like we've lost our best friends. It's the funniest picture you've ever seen."

I always like hearing stories about my mom and dad when they were little kids. I don't know why, I just do. "When did you and Dad stop fighting all the time?" I asked.

"Never, actually," said Aunt Margie. "We still argue to this day. But the arguing means something different now than it did back then. Now when we argue, it means that we love each other. We argue because it brings back old times. When we were kids, arguing just meant that we wanted to tear each other's heads off."

After dinner, we went back to Aunt Margie's house

and watched TV. The show we watched was an old black-and-white sitcom called *My Mother the Car*. It was about exactly what you would guess from the title—a guy whose mother is a car. It was the most ridiculous show I've ever seen.

My dad picked me up at nine o'clock and took me home.

Chapter 7

On Monday, a new edition of *The Kids' Club Book Service Newsletter* arrived at school. Miss Hufnagel allowed us to collect it from her desk after we had finished our science assignment, which was to color and label the parts of a leaf. I was good at labeling but not so good at coloring, so I always received a ✓ instead of a + on such assignments. This was okay with me. I was used to it. I finished the leaf assignment early and got to spend a good fifteen minutes looking through the newsletter before it was time for our vocabulary lesson. There was no listing for the *Secret Guide to North Mellwood*, which did not really surprise me. There was a listing for *101 Pickle Jokes*, though, and I decided to order it again. I also decided to order *A Wrinkle in Time* and a book of monster stickers called *The Round and the Furry*. Kevin Bugg told me at lunch that he was going to order *101 Pickle Jokes*, too, along with *The Hobbit* and a collection of Charlie Brown cartoons called *What's That Smell, Charlie Brown?* "That's how you got your *Secret Guide to North Mellwood*, right?" he said. "By ordering *101 Pickle Jokes*. Well, I want a copy for myself."

I wasn't so sure that that was the best way to get a copy, but I guessed it was worth a try. I couldn't imagine that *The Kids' Club Book Service Newsletter* actually sent the *Secret Guide to North Mellwood* to every single kid who happened to order *101 Pickle Jokes*. In fact, I assumed that I had gotten my copy through some sort of distribution error. But maybe Kevin Bugg was right and I was wrong. Anyway, the worst thing that could happen was that he would end up with a copy of *101 Pickle Jokes* instead, and that in itself was no bad thing

I stood behind Casey Robinson in the line for afternoon recess. "So are you going to tell me your big secret now?" she asked as we filed out together through the building.

"I'm going to do better than that," I said. "I'm going to show you."

"When?" she asked.

"This afternoon."

She fastened the metal snaps on her jacket. "You'd better," she said.

Our soccer game ended early that day when Lionel Beef kicked the soccer ball into the shopping center across the street. The playground at Larry Boone Elementary School was located right next to Mellwood Boulevard, one of the busiest streets in town. About once a week some kid would accidentally kick the soccer ball out of bounds, and it would go bouncing through all the traffic and end up rolling down to the Price Mart Supercenter. Nine times out of ten that kid was Lionel Beef. Usually someone would come driving up a few minutes later to return the ball to us, but not always. We lost a lot of soccer balls that way.

After school, Casey Robinson said to me, "All right, so what's the secret?"

We were gathering our books and stuff into our backpacks. "I'm going to have to show you," I said. "If I don't show you, you won't believe me." I waited until most of the other kids had left, and then I opened up the *Secret Guide to North Mellwood*. "Can you find your house on this map?"

"Is this the whole town?" said Casey Robinson. "Neat." She ran her fingers along the streets for a minute, pointing out the store where she went grocery shopping and the office building where her mom worked. Then she stopped at her house. "This is it," she said. "This is where I live. What does 'dolorifuge' mean?" That was the true name that was written over her house: DOLORIFUGE.

"I don't know," I said. "Okay, you go ahead and take the bus home, and I'll meet you at your house." I folded the map up and stuffed it into my backpack.

Casey Robinson looked irritated. "What do you mean, you'll meet me at my house? Why don't you ever want to ride the bus with me anymore?"

This took me by surprise. Casey was mad at me for some reason, and I didn't really understand why. It made me feel queasy and at the same time a little bit happy, and also embarrassed that I was a little bit happy. Basically, it made me feel confused. "I *do* want to ride the bus with you," I said. "But I can't today. Not if I'm going to show you the secret."

"Whatever," Casey Robinson said, and she stormed outside.

It took her about half an hour to arrive home, and by that time I was waiting for her on the front porch. I had transported straight into her kitchen, which was big and warm and lit by a long slanting skylight. I thought about sitting down to watch TV in the living room, but it seemed wrong to watch TV in somebody else's house when they didn't even know you were there.

I did help myself to a ginger ale out of the refrigerator, though.

In the living room, a yellow bird was rattling around inside a cage. I fed it a few sunflower seeds from a packet that I had in my lunchbox, and it ate the seeds right out of my fingers. Its beak made hard little pinches on my skin, but it didn't really hurt. There were pictures of Casey Robinson's family in the hallway leading to the front door. I looked at them as I headed outside. There was Casey with her mom and dad at Christmas, Casey being held up in the air by her older brother, Casey as a baby in a yellow dress. I unlocked the front door and stepped out onto the porch.

Casey got home about twenty minutes later, just as I was finishing my ginger ale. I could see that she was still a little bit mad at me. "How did you get here so fast?" she said.

"I transported."

"You what?"

"Take me into the kitchen and I'll show you," I said.

She shrugged her shoulders, sighed, and said, "Come on." I followed her inside. We crossed through the living room to get to the kitchen. "Hello, Judy," Casey said, tapping on the birdcage. "Hello, little bird." I threw my can of ginger ale in the trash can while she said something about how her mom must have forgotten to lock the door. "Now." She took her gloves off and tossed them onto the kitchen counter. "Enough is enough. Are you going to tell me what all this is about or what?"

"Okay," I said. "Dolorifuge."

And I was standing by the statue of Larry Boone. I looked around. Nobody was there. A soft wind was blowing a brown paper bag across the ground, and the shadow of a cloud was passing through the parking lot. I knocked three times in the hollow of the statue's knee. "Dolorifuge," I said again, and I was standing in Casey Robinson's kitchen.

She had dropped her books onto the floor, and her eyes were filled with tears. Her mouth was wide open in shock. I had heard about people's mouths opening in shock, but I had never actually seen it happen before. Her voice came out in a hoarse whisper. "You can disappear."

"Not disappear," I said. "Transport." I took the *Secret Guide to North Mellwood* from my backpack and spread it out on the kitchen floor. "And this is how," I said.

I explained to Casey Robinson where the book had come from and how it worked. I told her about *101 Pickle Jokes*, and the true names, and the five hidden portals. She was shaking her head back and forth. "I told you you wouldn't believe me unless I showed you," I said. I folded the map up and put it away. "Here, take my hand. This won't work unless you're holding on to me."

Casey Robinson took my hand right away, but I couldn't tell whether it was because she believed me or because she was still in shock from seeing me vanish and reappear in her kitchen. Her grip was strong. Her fingers were shaking. "Dolorifuge," I said.

We were standing in the courtyard of Larry Boone Elementary School.

Casey Robinson let go of my hand and took two steps back. Her face seemed to wrinkle up as she looked around. At first I thought she was going to cry—that's what it looked like—but then she gave a big smile and started to giggle. Buckets of laughter just came rolling out of her. "This is great!" she said. "I can't believe it!" I was smiling myself, she was so excited. Even though she had let go, I could still feel the pressure of her fingers on my hand.

"I told you," I said.

We spent the next half hour or so transporting to various places around town—the newsstand, the Burger Barn, the North Mellwood Shopping Mall. It was fun, but really it just felt good to be spending so much time with

Casey Robinson. It was as if we were secret partners and nobody else in the world mattered. Once or twice, the two of us landed in a place where people were watching. You'd think we would have scared the pants off those people, the way we appeared right in front of them, but they always just tossed their heads around like they were trying to shoo a bug away and ended up looking someplace else. I guess they thought we had been there all along and they just hadn't been paying enough attention. No matter how strange the world gets, people will always find a way to explain it to themselves.

It was almost evening when we returned to the statue of Larry Boone. Casey Robinson wrinkled up her nose. "Something smells horrible," she said.

"Yeah, I know," I said. "I'm not sure what that is. It happens every time I use the portal, but it usually goes away after a few seconds." She didn't say anything.

"Well," I said after a minute, "we should probably go home now." I didn't really want to leave yet, but I knew that we should. "We don't want our parents to come looking for us."

Casey Robinson stopped me, grabbing hold of my jacket. "Wait," she said. "I want to try one quick experiment before we go, okay? First, let's both knock on the statue." I nodded. We both knocked on the statue, and then Casey Robinson took my hand.

"All right, now you say one true name and I'll say another—at exactly the same time. Don't let go, and we'll see what happens."

"All right," I said, and I squeezed her hand. "On the count of three then. One, two, three—"

"Guddle," I said.

"Dolorifuge," said Casey Robinson.

And something very strange happened. It was as if we were standing in two different places at the same time. At first I thought we were both in my living room— Rhubarb was napping on the television, and I could see the blue spines of my dad's Oxford English Dictionary lined up on the bookshelf. But when I looked around I realized that I could also see the skylight in Casey Robinson's kitchen ceiling, and her yellow bird Judy in her birdcage. I looked behind us. I could see the hallway leading to Casey Robinson's front door, and in exactly the same place I could see my own backyard. They were superimposed on top of each other (this was one of our vocabulary words for the week: *superimposed*), like two film slides in the same slot of a film carousel. Neither one looked quite real. Casey's living-room couch was on top of my dad's desk. My downstairs bathroom was in the middle of her driveway.

"This is creepy," said Casey Robinson.

"No kidding," I said.

I don't know why, but I decided to reach down and pet Rhubarb. My hand passed right through her. Her back tensed, and she twitched her head toward me, and an angry hissing noise came from her throat. It was unlike any noise I've ever heard her make before. We took a few steps backward to get away from Rhubarb and ended up walking into, and then *inside of*, my dad's easy chair and Casey Robinson's kitchen counter. I don't know how to describe this. It was as if the shapes in our houses were made entirely out of water: we could feel their weight on all sides of us, but this did not keep us from moving around inside them. Casey Robinson was the only thing I could feel that was completely solid.

"I don't like this," she said. "Let's get back to the statue, Howie."

"I agree," I said. "Let's go. One, two, three—

"Guddle," I said.

"Dolorifuge," said Casey Robinson.

The courtyard of our elementary school blinked back into sight.

For at least five minutes, we just stood there looking at each other. The sun was sinking behind the school building. A brisk wind was rattling the chain on the flagpole. Finally, Casey Robinson exhaled loudly and let go of my hand. I saw a shiver travel across her shoulders. "I don't ever want to do that again," she said. And at exactly the same moment, I said the very same thing.

Chapter

My mom works as a physician's assistant at the North Mellwood City Hospital. A physician's assistant is a lot like a nurse, except that nurses have to work the same crazy hours that doctors do, and physician's assistants get to keep a regular schedule. My mom works from nine to five, Monday through Friday, and every other weekend. Most people picture nurses wearing clean white outfits with red crosses on their hats, but the clothes my mom wears to work look like a pair of blue pajamas. My dad is a product design coordinator for a novelty gift company. This means that he invents things like Whoopee Cushions and Joy Buzzers. Actually, Whoopee Cushions and Joy Buzzers were invented before my dad was old enough to start working there, but he did invent a few things you might have heard of. He invented a kind of soap that turns your hands black when you wash them. He also invented a type of chewing gum with a candy center that moves like a real bug when you bite into it. Lately, he has been working on something called Misfortune Cookies. Misfortune

Cookies are just like regular fortune cookies, except that all the fortunes they contain are bad. For example, if you crack open one of my dad's cookies, you might read:

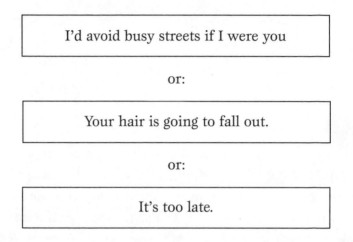

> I'd avoid busy streets if I were you

or:

> Your hair is going to fall out.

or:

> It's too late.

On the back of the fortune slips is a list of unlucky numbers. This list is always the same:

13	13	13	13	13
	13	13	13	

My dad also works Monday through Friday from nine to five—just like my mom. They don't get to spend too much time alone together. On evenings and weekends, I'm always right there in the house with them, and when they go out on a date together, they always have to be home by eight or nine o'clock to pay the babysitter. This means that when I ask to spend the night with a friend of mine, as long as it's not a school night, they almost always say yes.

That Saturday night, I spent the night with Kevin Bugg.

The best part about spending the night with somebody is being able to sneak out together in the dark after everyone else is asleep. (The *worst* part about spending the night with somebody is trying to fall asleep on the floor between a pair of old blankets.) It was past midnight when the Buggs turned their lights off and went to bed. We waited until we heard them snoring. Then Kevin Bugg and I took the bicycles from his garage and pedaled into town. We were headed for the elementary school and the statue of Larry Boone, and from there to Star Systems Video Parlor, the arcade that Mr. Bugg operates.

Kevin Bugg lives much closer to school than I do, and it didn't take us long to get there. We followed a shortcut he knew that ran behind a Tae Kwon Do studio and through a patch of woods. Then we rode straight down Mellwood Boulevard to the school. There were almost no cars out, and it was strange to see the traffic lights turning green and red and yellow with nobody driving on the road. From the school we transported directly into the video parlor. We landed behind an old Q*Bert machine. The video games all around us were were making bleeping and punching noises, and they filled the room with a flickering blue light. Mr. Bugg leaves the video games running overnight because if you turn them off, you erase the list of winning scores from the machines. The list of winning scores is kind of a big deal. It's always disappointing to find that your name has been erased and some other kid with a lower score than you has taken your spot. Mr. Bugg knew that this was a fast way to lose customers. Sometimes, on Saturday mornings, before Star Systems opens, a row of kids will line up out on the sidewalk and just stare inside at the video games, fogging the windows up with their breath. There is nothing more exciting than the sight of all those screens— all the aliens and karate sounds and flashing INSERT COIN signs. It's like the Christmas gift displays you see in the windows of department stores: they make you want the toys so much more than you normally would, because they're right there in front of you and you just can't get to them.

"This is so cool," I said as Kevin Bugg and I stepped out from behind the Q*Bert machine.

Kevin Bugg was nervous. He was walking around on tiptoes and speaking in whispers. "My dad would kill me if he knew we were in here. We have to be very careful."

"Don't worry," I said. "Now where are the tokens?"

"We don't need any," Kevin Bugg said. He went behind the back counter and fished a key out from one of the drawers. "This key opens all the video games," he said. "All you have to do is flip a switch inside, and you can play all you want." He opened the change cabinet of a Galaga machine and flipped the silver toggle inside. A sign flashed onto the screen: SELECT ONE PLAYER OR TWO.

"Awesome," I said. "Let's play."

My all-time favorite video game is called Mutant

Shadow Boxers II. In Mutant Shadow Boxers II, you get to control two different fighters: one of them is a regular human being, and the other one is his shadow. Both the regular human being and the shadow go from screen to screen fighting other Mutant Shadow Boxers. The trick is that the regular human being is actually a mutant, so his shadow isn't a normal shadow, it's a mutant shadow. Some of the shadows look like animals—grizzly bears, lions, crocodiles, that sort of thing—and some of them look like monsters or dinosaurs or aliens. It depends on which character you choose to play. My favorite character, for instance, has a Bigfoot shadow, and Kevin Bugg's favorite character has a giant snake shadow. The shadows can throw punches and fight, and they can even die just like a real person.

I spent the next few hours playing Mutant Shadow Boxers II. I was playing as well as I've ever played in my life. Every time I got killed, I would continue the game where I left off by pressing the button on the front panel, so my score just kept adding up. Kevin Bugg played against me for a few matches, then he wandered off and played Ski Slalom for a while. Finally he just got bored and stood behind my shoulder watching me play. "Look out!" he said, and "Here comes another one!" and "Use the Bigfoot! Use the Bigfoot!" Every so often, I would take a look at my score. It was in the tens of millions, higher than I had ever scored before, and higher than I had ever even *seen* anybody score. By the time my wrist got too tired to play, my score was over 37 million—an amazing number.

I entered my name on the list of winning scores: HOWIEQUACKENBUS, it read (there was only room for fifteen letters).

"Wow!" said Kevin Bugg. He looked at the list again and did a double take. "Holy smokes! You beat Mike Channering!"

"I sure did," I said. Mike Channering was positioned at number two on the list of winning scores. I was number one.

"You don't understand!" said Kevin Bugg. "Nobody beats Mike Channering!" It was true. Kevin Bugg showed me the display of winning scores on the Indy 500 Racer machine, which was right next to Mutant Shadow Boxers II. Mike Channering's name was at the top of the list. In fact, Mike Channering's name was at the top of every list we looked at. On the older games, the ones that were not able to display his full name, there were just his two initials—M-space-C. But there seemed to be no doubt that it was him. "He has the number one score on every machine in this arcade," said Kevin Bugg.

"Not anymore," I said.

Kevin Bugg smiled. "He's gonna freak." All of a sudden, his smile turned into a yawn. He looked at his watch. "You don't want to play anymore, do you?"

"Are you kidding?" I said. "My wrist is killing me." I thought of something: "Hey, your dad won't notice my score, will he? Maybe we'd better erase it."

"The only way to erase it is to unplug the machine," Kevin Bugg said. "But I wouldn't worry about it. My dad never really reads the scores himself. He doesn't care about that sort of thing."

"Okay," I said. "We'd better get going, then."

We squeezed ourselves behind the Q*Bert machine, said "hurdy-gurdy," and transported to the statue of Larry Boone. Then we rode our bikes back to Kevin Bugg's place. The streets were even quieter than before, but the traffic lights were still changing color every few seconds—red and green and yellow. I noticed that so late at night, the lights stayed yellow longer than they stayed either red or green.

We returned the bicycles to the garage and crept back inside. Mr. and Mrs. Bugg were sound asleep in their beds. I followed Kevin Bugg through the dark to his room. We didn't even brush our teeth or change into our pajamas. In fact, I was so satisfied with my video-gamesmanship that I fell straight to sleep as soon as I hit the floor.

Chapter 9

It didn't take long for the word to spread that I had beaten Mike Channering's high score on Mutant Shadow Boxers II. Kids were coming up to me on the playground and congratulating me. "Good work, Howie!" they said.

"Way to go, Howie!"

"Boy, you've got some nerve, Howie!"

That afternoon, as I was walking to the bus with Casey Robinson, somebody jostled me from behind and made me drop my backpack. The zipper split open, and my books went sliding out. I accidentally kicked one down the sidewalk a few feet before I could stop walking, which left a gray scrape of cardboard across the back cover. As I was picking the books up, a shadow fell over me. I looked up to see a kid in a green army jacket. He was one of the biggest kids I've ever seen. He had straight black hair that fell across his eyes, and there were already patches of stubble on his jaw and his neck. He stepped on my social studies book. "You'd better watch it, kid," he said. Then he stomped away into the parking lot.

"Who was that?" I said.

"Don't you know?" Casey Robinson said. "That was Mike Channering."

Mike Channering, it turns out, was in the sixth grade at Larry Boone Elementary School. I had seen him around before, but I hadn't known his name, and I had never spoken to him. (Nobody in the fifth grade ever spoke to anyone in the sixth grade. In fact, nobody in any grade ever really spoke to anybody in any other grade. You might talk to your brother or sister, but otherwise it just wasn't done.) Mike Channering had been transferred into Larry Boone Elementary School earlier that year, and I heard that he had been left back a few times. He had a reputation as a tough guy, and people said he had been expelled from his other school. Nobody could remember ever seeing him get in a fight, but still, people tried to stay on his good side. Also, he was a fanatic video game player. He had apparently spent all of Sunday afternoon at Star Systems Video Parlor trying to top my score on Mutant Shadow Boxers II, but he hadn't been able to.

I had more important things to worry about than Mike Channering, though. It was almost Valentine's Day, and I still hadn't decorated my shoebox. Miss Hufnagel had asked us to bring shoebox mailboxes to school for the Valentine's Day card exchange. Most of the kids wrapped their shoeboxes in pink or red wrapping paper and just glued a few heart shapes on here and there, but a few kids always put in the extra effort to make a really special mailbox. The teachers would award ribbons to the best mailboxes in each class. My friend Nathaniel Hawthorne always won first place for our class. Nathaniel Hawthorne is a talented artist. He's ten years old, like me, but he can paint pictures that look as good as anything you've seen on a wall. He decorates his Valentine's Day mailboxes with swirls of color on the sides, and on the top he usually paints six or seven Cupids with strips of cloth covering their private parts.

That evening, my dad helped me decorate my shoebox. "Why don't you wrap it in Christmas paper?" he said. "I bet none of the other kids will do that." But I had a better idea. I drew a big mouth around the mail slot, with fangs and tonsils and a bright red tongue. Above the mouth I drew a monster face. It was green and had checkerboard eyes and a long white horn in the middle of its nose. We cut up an old brown wig my dad had worn one year for Halloween and pasted it around the sides for fur. Then my dad molded a pair of arms and legs out of foil and helped me glue them on. By the time I finished, it was a pretty good mailbox. I knew that I wouldn't beat Nathaniel Hawthorne, but I thought I might get second place. Miss Hufnagel would think that my mailbox showed a lot of creativity. Also, I used lots of aluminum foil. Teachers go crazy for aluminum foil.

The next night, we bought a box of valentines at the supermarket. I needed twenty-one cards, twenty for my classmates and one for Miss Hufnagel. I picked a box of Flaxman Greenman cards. Flaxman Greenman is a basketball player. His cards have messages on them like I'D JUMP A MILE FOR YOU and YOU'RE A PURE-D SLAM DUNK and LET'S TAKE IT TO THE HOOP. On most of the cards I just signed my name—Howie—but on Casey Robinson's card I thought I should write something special. I couldn't decide what to say, though. "You're the prettiest girl I know"? "I enjoy riding the bus with you"? "I kind of want to kiss you"? In the end I just wrote, "Love, Howie," and left it at that. I halfway hoped that she wouldn't notice the love part.

Our Valentine's Day party was on a Friday. It was one of those sunny spring days that appear in the middle of February and fool you into thinking that winter is over. The thing to remember is that winter is never over: the clouds will always sweep back in and drop some more snow. The school bus let us off in front of the building and we walked inside. My valentines were in the pocket of my backpack, and I was carrying my shoebox in my arms. "That thing is gross," Susan Goins said.

"It's a monster," I said. "I made it with my dad."

"What *is* that on the sides—hair!?" she asked.

"It's part of an old wig," I said.

Susan Goins shuddered.

As I was heading through the door, someone knocked the shoebox from my hands. It tumbled over and landed on the floor. I heard the crumpling sound before I saw what happened. When I looked down, I saw a big black shoe on top of a mound of brown wig. My Valentine's

Day mailbox was crushed flat. At first I just felt a hollow feeling in my stomach, but after a second or two, I became boiling mad. The big black shoe belonged to Mike Channering, and he was smiling.

"I can't believe you did that!" I yelled. "You jerk!"

"Now we're even," Mike Channering said.

"Even?" I said. "You crushed my mailbox!"

He shrugged and started to clomp away down the hall in his big black shoes. I was furious. "You . . . turd!" I shouted. I don't know why I said that word in particular— I couldn't think what else to say—but by the way he stopped in his tracks, I could see that it had gotten to him.

He turned to face me. "Tomorrow," he said. "Twelve o'clock. Either we fight or we race."

"I'm not going to fight you," I said. "You're twice as big as I am."

Mike Channering smirked. "Then we race," he said. "Star Systems to Super Crazy Prices. Meet me at noon."

That afternoon, I tried my best to repair the damage that had been done to my mailbox, but it was no use. The arms and legs had been pressed into flat pieces of aluminum foil that didn't look like arms or legs at all. The wig had come unglued from the sides of the box and was beginning to smell funny. There was a big dirty shoeprint in the middle of the monster's face. It was a perfect mess.

"Tough love, huh?" said Miss Hufnagel when she saw the box. A crestfallen look must have come over my face, because she swallowed her laughter all of a sudden and said, "Oh, I'm sorry, Howie. Somebody did this to you, didn't they? Here, let me see." I turned over the shoe-box to her. She pushed her hand against the inside of it until she had forced it into a roughly boxlike shape, but it still wasn't the same.

At the end of the day, we drank punch and ate cup-cakes and exchanged our valentines. I was feeling better by then. The slot on my mailbox was so crooked that everyone in my class had to fold their cards in half and wiggle them back and forth in order to fit them inside. It was really kind of funny. After everyone had delivered their valentines to the boxes, Miss Hufnagel allowed us to take them to our desks and open them.

Casey Robinson watched me from a few seats over as I opened hers. It was an Animal Kingdom card. On the front was a picture of a dolphin poking its head up from the water. It looked like it was smiling—though who knows if dolphins can smile. On the back of the card it said, "We get along swimmingly," and beneath that Casey had written her name: "Love, Casey." When I shook the envelope, a candy heart fell out onto my desk. I LOVE YOU, it read.

I still haven't eaten it.

Chapter 10

I woke up late Saturday morning. My mom was in the kitchen preparing bacon and eggs. I could smell the food cooking all the way from my bedroom, and I could hear it sizzling in the pan as I went downstairs. "Well hello, sleepyhead," my mom said. She mussed my hair. "Would you like me to fix you some breakfast?"

"No, thanks," I said. "I'll just get some cereal." I like breakfast food—eggs and bacon and stuff like that—but I'm never very hungry when I wake up in the morning. I usually just eat a bowl of cereal. Breakfast food is best at night, I think. I remember one night when my parents let me stay up late watching a movie with them on TV. The movie was called *The Eyes of March*, and it was about an emperor named March who lives on a planet where all the people have six eyes. The eyes grow on stalks and sort of wave around in the air whenever anyone wants to look

at something. I don't know how a person could see anything at all with his eyes waving around like that. Anyway,
it was almost midnight when the movie ended. The living
room was perfectly quiet after we turned the TV off. We
should have been ready to go to bed, but we were all
suddenly starving. We could hear each other's stomachs
making these bearlike growling noises. "Is anybody
hungry?" my dad said. We all laughed. We went to the
kitchen and made scrambled eggs and bacon and sausage
and pancakes and toast, and we poured three big glasses
of orange juice for ourselves. It was one in the morning
by the time we finished stuffing our mouths with all
the food we had prepared. That was the best meal I've
ever eaten in my life.

I poured myself a bowl of cereal and sat down on the
couch to watch cartoons. Rhubarb curled up beside me,
and when I finished eating my cereal, I let her lap the milk
from the bowl. I could hear the shower running upstairs
whenever the TV went quiet. My dad came down a few
minutes later smelling of soap. He gave my mom an aston-
ished look when he saw how much food she had on her
plate. "Hungry, Sylvia?" he asked.

"I'm eating for two," she said, and patted her belly. By
this time she was almost eight months pregnant, and her
stomach was as round as a globe.

I was supposed to meet Mike Channering at twelve
o'clock outside the video arcade. At eleven, I told my
parents that I was going out for a while. I rode to Larry
Boone Elementary School on my bike. From there I trans-

ported to the Critz & Co. Movie Memorabilia Shop, and from there I walked up the street to Star Systems Video Parlor.

By then it was almost noon. A bunch of kids from my school were milling around on the sidewalk, and others came streaming out of the arcade when they saw that I was there. I saw Kevin Bugg and Casey Robinson and most of the rest of my class. Also, there were some kids I had never spoken to before, kids that I recognized from the bus or the playground. Some of them were Mike Channering's friends, but plenty of them were just there to see the race. A few of the people who had come were under the impression that there was going to be a fight. "When's the fight start?" one of them asked me, and I said, "Twelve o'clock—but it's a race, not a fight." There were several loud groans, and a few of the kids walked back inside the arcade.

"Where's the finish line?" somebody else asked me.

"The Super Crazy Prices Convenience Store," I said.

A bunch of the kids jumped on their bikes and rode off in that direction.

"Who's Howie Quackenbush?" one kid said, and I told him that I was. He sized me up. "Boy," he said, shaking his head, "you don't have a chance, do you?"

Mike Channering showed up a few minutes later. He was wearing his green canvas army jacket and his big black tennis shoes. It looked like he hadn't been able to shave that morning—there were hairy places all over his chin and neck. A buzz of impatience went up from the kids who were waiting. "Are you ready, Quackenbus?" Mike Channering said.

"It's Quacken*bush*," I said. "There's only room for fifteen letters on the video game, so—"

"Whatever," Mike Channering said. He didn't have a cigarette in his hand, but he looked like he had just taken a puff from one and flicked it aside, if you know what I mean. He tossed his jacket to a red-haired friend of his. "From here to Super Crazy Prices," said Mike Channering. "We'll start on the count of three."

"Who's going to count?" I said.

"I don't care." Mike Channering looked around at the crowd. "How about him—that fat friend of yours?" He pointed to Kevin Bugg.

In a tiny voice, Kevin Bugg said, "It's glandular."

"Okay, 'Glandular,'" Mike Channering said. "Count off for us."

Mike Channering and I took runners' stances behind one of the cracks on the sidewalk. I could feel my heart drumming in my chest. But I wasn't too worried—I had a plan. "One . . . two . . . three . . . go!" said Kevin Bugg, and we launched ourselves into the race.

Mike Channering was faster than me—I could tell that as soon as we started running. I was sprinting as hard as I could just to keep up with him. Behind me I heard the shouts of the kids outside Star Systems, and beside me I heard the slapping of his feet on the ground. We rounded the first corner of the race, and I let him pull ahead of me a few paces. He couldn't see me, but he could hear me close behind him, so he kept pushing himself to run faster. We were approaching Critz & Co. Movie Memorabilia Shop—the store where I had transported just before the race. When we got there I ducked beneath the awning, said the store's true name, and transported back to the elementary school. I was panting for breath, and I took a minute to rest against the statue of Larry Boone. So far, so good, I thought. Then I said, "Megaflop," and transported to the Byte-Sized Computer Store, which was just around the corner from Super Crazy Prices. I began to run. One of the kids who was waiting at the finish line caught sight of me, and then another, and another. I heard a cheer rise up from the crowd.

"Oh, my gosh," said a voice as I neared the end of the race. "I think that's Howie Quackenbush!"

"It can't be," said somebody else—but it was. I pounded across the finish line and stood there trying to catch my breath as people slapped me on the back. I was doubled over with my hands on my knees. Mike Channering followed about thirty seconds later, running as hard as he could. He was pumping his arms as he neared the finish line, but the closer he got, the more confused he looked. He slowed to a trot as he caught my eye. "Tough break, Mike," someone said. "Maybe next time," another kid said.

Mike Channering gave me a shove. "You cheated, Quackenbus," he said. "I don't know how, but you cheated." I could see the other kids, the ones who had been standing at the beginning line of the race, approaching from up the street. They were riding their bikes and running down the sidewalk, shouting, "Who won? Who won? Who won?" One of the first kids to get there was Mike Channering's red-haired friend. Mike grabbed his jacket from him and slung it over his shoulder. "You cheated, kid," he said again, pointing his finger at me and shaking his head. Then he pushed his way through the crowd and stalked away.

I suppose I should have felt bad. Mike Channering was right, after all: I had cheated. But that part of it—the feeling bad—didn't come until later. Just then, I was enjoying my victory. All the kids were shaking my hand and saying things like, "I didn't know you had it in you," and "Way to go, Howie." There was a warm humming sensation in my body, and my legs felt kind of balloony, as if they were ready to float away. After a while most of the kids drifted off in little clusters, to the park or the arcade or their homes, and it was just me and a few of the people from my class. I led them up the street toward the elementary school.

"Where are we going, anyway?" said Casey Goss, the boy Casey.

"To Larry Boone," I said. "That's where I left my bike."

Casey Robinson and Kevin Bugg gave each other a look.

Chapter 11

Mike Channering did not stop bothering me after the race. I had thought that he would. For some reason, I imagined that if I beat him in the race, I would never have to deal with him again. I should have known better. He never actually hurt me—or never *really* hurt me—but he pushed me around every chance he got. I had to be extra careful when I was at school or he would dump the books from my hands, knock me into a wall, hike my pants up from behind, and throw chewing gum into my hair. All the other kids in my class knew what was going on and helped me to watch out for him, but he was pretty sneaky for a guy so big. I thought about telling Miss Hufnagel or the principal, but my gut instinct told me that it would just make things worse. The last thing I needed was for Mike Channering to get suspended from school or something and then blame it on me.

I don't know why I decided to transport to his house. Somehow it seemed like a good idea at the time. Maybe I thought I could talk him into leaving me alone. Maybe I wanted to frighten him (though I was careful not to let him see me when I actually got there). Or maybe I was just looking for some kind of ammunition to use against him. For whatever reason, the next Saturday afternoon, while my parents were out shopping for a stroller, I went downstairs to the television, said a quick "guddle," and transported to the statue of Larry Boone. I had been transporting back and forth from there every four hours since I had finished school on Friday. It turned out that that was about how long the portal effect was good for—four hours—and I wanted to keep it in operation. I wasn't lazy or a portal junkie or anything like that. I just knew that I was going to need the portal to get to Mike Channering's house the next day.

It had snowed again the night before, and the school grounds were covered with three or four inches of dry white powder. The cars and kids and buses and such had not had a chance to track it up and turn it into brown mush yet, so everything still looked clean and beautiful. I looked up Mike Channering's house in the *Secret Guide to North Mellwood*. Its true name was MUNDUNGUS. I felt a little bit nervous. What if I landed on his roof, or directly in his lap or something like that? But I went ahead and knocked in the hollow of Larry Boone's knee and said the true name: "Mundungus."

At first I couldn't tell where I was. It was pitch dark,

and my breathing sounded much louder than it had before. I could feel something soft and ticklish brushing against my face. I stretched my arms out in front of me, and they bumped against a wall. I stretched them out again, to both sides, and they bumped against two more walls. I turned around. There was a crack of light reaching up from the floor to the ceiling. That's when I realized—I was in a closet.

I listened to make sure I couldn't hear anybody talking or moving around, and then I pushed the door open a couple of inches. I put my eye to the gap. Outside there was a bed with a small hill of clothing on it and a stereo with a stack of CDs and two cabinet-sized speakers. On the desk in the corner of the room, there was a mound of quarters along with a few school books and some airplane glue. The walls were covered with posters of hard rock bands with names like Death Comes for the Archbishop and Hide the Knives and The Skinless. And on the floor I could see a pair of big black tennis shoes. Not only was I in a closet—I was in the closet of Mike Channering's bedroom.

I poked my head out. The bedroom door was open, but nobody was there, so it seemed safe enough to come out. That's what I did: I stepped outside. I could hear voices coming from somewhere else in the house—it sounded like people were either arguing with each other or watching TV. When I was little, my parents used to throw the food we didn't eat, along with the leaves they raked and the grass they cut, into a big wire pen in our backyard. They called it a compost heap. Mike Channering's room smelled a little like that compost heap. It wasn't a bad smell—just old. I began to snoop around, walking quietly so that no one would hear me. The quarters on Mike Channering's desk were for video games, I guessed. There was also a notepad on the desk with the words "Mutant Shadow Boxers II" written on it, and beneath that was written: "Quackenbus—high score 37 million. Channering—high score ~~17 million~~ ~~19 million~~ 20½ million." When I saw what was on top of Mike Channering's dresser, I dropped the notepad right onto the floor. He had an Eggbot! It was one of the new ones that I don't have yet, Maximus Seed, who can shoot missiles out of his wrists in robot form and flap his wings in chicken form. On the floor by the bed was a pair of pajamas, and I bent over to take a look at them. They were a light green color, with a darker green around the cuffs and the collar, and they had a picture of the Incredible Hulk on the front. The Incredible Hulk was punching through a brick wall, and there was a speech bubble saying "Hulk smash!" coming from his mouth. Best of all, the pajamas were the type with nylon feet sewn into the bottom. This was perfect! If I was looking for ammunition to use against Mike Channering, I couldn't ask for anything better.

I was trying to decide what to do with the pajamas when I heard footsteps coming down the hallway. I thought about making a dash for the closet, but it was too far away. Instead, I crawled under the bed and listened to the footsteps coming closer. I lay there as quietly as I could and watched Mike Channering's feet walking across the floor. They stopped by the bed, not six inches from my face, and then the mattress sank and I felt the bedsprings scratching against my cheek. It was really uncomfortable. I hoped that Mike Channering wasn't planning to take a nap.

A minute later another set of footsteps came beating down the hallway—I could hear them really well with my ear pressed to the floor—and stopped at the bedroom door.

"What do you want now?" said Mike Channering. I recognized his voice.

"What do I want?" said the other person. He cleared his throat and spat noisily, and the spit landed right on the floor. I couldn't believe it. Then he spoke in a deep grumble. "This room is a pigsty. One more bit of filth won't make a difference, will it?" He waited for an answer. "Will it?" he repeated.

"I guess not," Mike Channering said. Mike Channering didn't sound mean or angry like he did at school. He just sounded tired. "Will you leave me alone now?"

"What's the matter?" taunted the other man. "Is Mr. Tough Guy gonna cry? Is little Mikey gonna wet his pants?"

Mike Channering didn't speak.

"You make me sick," said the other man. He didn't yell or anything—he just stated it as if it were a matter of fact. "We never should've had you, you know that?

Your mother and I . . . we never should've had you." He paused for a moment. "You little turd," he said, and then he walked away.

Mike Channering gave a long, quiet sigh.

I felt sick to my stomach. If I had been in the closet, I would have transported straight back to the statue of Larry Boone. That's what I wanted to do. I was too far away, though, for the portal to work. I knew that.

I tested it anyway. "Mundungus," I said, whispering as quietly as I could. Nothing happened.

I waited under the bed for more than an hour. Every time I thought Mike Channering had fallen asleep, he would mumble something to himself or get up and walk around the room for a minute. I was afraid that if I waited there too much longer, the effect of the portal would wear off, but I knew that I couldn't just crawl out from under the bed without being spotted. There was no telling what Mike Channering would do if he found out I had been hiding from him in his own room. Eventually, I decided that I should just make a run for the closet. He would see me, of course, but I was sure that he wouldn't be able to reach me in time. I was just about to make my move when an idea came to me.

The notepad that I had dropped from the desk was still lying on the floor. I thought that I could reach it without moving too far. Cautiously, I stretched my arm out from under the bed, and when my hand touched the notepad, I pulled it back to me. There was an ink pen clipped to the top. I uncapped it and wrote a note:

Meet me at midnight by the statue outside Larry Boone Elementary School. Come alone. I'll explain everything to you. P.S. This isn't a trick.

Sincerely, Howie Quackenbush.

Then I removed the top sheet of paper from the note-pad, tearing it carefully so that Mike Channering wouldn't hear me. I planned to climb out from under the bed, throw the note at him, and dash straight into the closet. He would be so surprised that he would never catch me before I transported. And maybe my note would interest him enough that he wouldn't want to beat me up. It wasn't a great plan, but it wasn't too shabby, either. But when I slid out from under the bed, I found Mike Channering fast asleep. His eyes were giving little flickers behind his eyelids, and his stomach was rising slowly up and down. I placed the note I had written on his pillow and walked to the open closet.

"Mundungus," I said, and I was standing in the snow outside the elementary school.

That night, around 11:45, I got out of bed and changed into a pair of jeans and a heavy shirt. I slipped on some shoes and buttoned up my winter coat. Then I transported to the statue of Larry Boone. The sky had cleared and there was a full moon out. The only footprints I could see on the ground were my own, and they were standing right there beside the statue. The rest of the snow was still perfectly smooth. The air was freezing. Within seconds, my teeth were chattering and I was shivering all over. I was so cold that I could actually feel the shape of my bones in my body: I mean, I knew where the bones ended and the muscles began. Maybe my bones felt the cold and my muscles didn't, or maybe it was the other way around—I don't know. Anyway, I don't think I've ever been so cold in my life. I wasn't sure whether Mike Channering was even going to show up, but I was determined to wait for him.

After a minute or two, I spotted him coming across the schoolyard. His hands were buried in the pockets of his army jacket, but other than that he looked like he didn't even notice the cold. I could see his footprints clearly in the moonlight. The tracks he left in the snow looked like a zipper.

I expected him to be angry, or, if not angry, at least his usual grouchy self. But instead he just stopped beside me and nodded his head. He acted like he'd been out for a stroll in the middle of the night and just happened to bump into me there. I guess he was different when there weren't any other kids around. "Hey," he said.

"Hey. Did you have any trouble getting away from home?" I asked. My teeth were chattering.

"Nah." He shrugged. "Nobody cares what I do. Look, what's all this about?"

"I'm going to have to show you," I said. I knocked three times on the statue of Larry Boone. Mike Channering looked at me like I was some kind of lunatic. I grabbed hold of his shoulder, and he started to cock his arm back. Then, before he could punch me, I said, "Hurdy-gurdy."

We were standing in the video arcade behind the

Q*Bert machine. Mike Channering stumbled back and tripped over the extension cord. It came unplugged. The speakers on the machine gave a high-pitched *dit* as it shut down. "What are you, magic or something?" Mike Channering said.

"Not exactly," I said. "It's kind of a long story," and I told him all about the portals and the list of true names and the *Secret Guide to North Mellwood*. At first I thought he wouldn't believe me—in fact, I was still a little worried he was going to punch me—but he just nodded like he had finally figured something out.

"So that's how you beat me in the race," he said. "I knew it had to be some kind of trick."

"Well, sorry about that," I said. "But I've got something that I bet will make up for it. Come on." At that, I got the master key from behind the back counter and unlocked the change cabinet of Mutant Shadow Boxers II. Mike Channering followed me. We were leaving wavy lines of snow on the floor from the treads on the bottom of our shoes. I flipped the toggle inside Mutant Shadow Boxers II, and the SELECT ONE PLAYER OR TWO flashed onto the screen. "This is how I scored so high," I said. "You can keep playing until you get tired of it. No quarters necessary."

Mike Channering's face lit up. I had never seen him look happy before. "Are you serious?" he said.

"Give it a try," I said.

He muscled up to the video game and ran his hands over the control panel. He looked like I look when I'm pet-

76

ting Rhubarb. He pressed the start button, and the machine made a blooping noise. Then he began to play. I had never witnessed anything like it. Mike Channering was without a doubt the best, quickest, most skillful video-game player I have ever seen in my life. His hands were all over the place. The arcade was empty, but even if it had been packed with customers, I was certain that everybody in the place would be doing exactly what I was doing— gathering around that machine and watching Mike Channering play. The shadow of his mutant shadow boxer, a tarantula, kept growing faster and faster, bigger and bigger, and in a little more than an hour, he had beaten my score of 37 million. He was fighting against two or three different mutant shadow boxers at a time, and trouncing them. He finally stopped playing at 51 million. "I guess that's enough for tonight," he said, stepping back from the machine. He laced his fingers together and pushed them out, cracking his knuckles. "We can go whenever you're ready."

"That was amazing," I said. I shook my head. I was truly in awe. "You're the best player I've ever seen in my life."

Mike Channering gave a tiny smile. "Thanks, Quack-enbus," he said. "You know, you're all right." He boxed my shoulder with his fist. It hurt a little, but I knew he was trying to be nice, so I didn't complain.

I shut the change cabinet and returned the key to the back counter. Before we left, I plugged the Q*Bert machine back in. Mike Channering played a single game on it, on his own quarter, just to place his name on the screen. I've never been any good at Q*Bert. I always hop right off the edge of the pyramid and fall to my death—this happens pretty much every time I play. Mike Channering, of course, was outstanding. He finished playing after about half an hour, and we slid behind the machine and returned to Larry Boone Elementary School.

Chapter 12

My mom and dad were a little bit worried about me. "You've seemed pretty tired lately," they said to me. This was a few weeks after Mike Channering and I spent the night at Star Systems. "Is anything wrong?" they asked. The truth was that I had been hopping around town every night with Kevin Bugg or Casey Robinson, or Kevin Bugg *and* Casey Robinson, and I was not getting very much sleep. After dark I'd transport to the statue, go pick them up, and then off we'd go. One day, I actually fell asleep in class. I had seen other kids do this before, but it had never happened to me personally. I woke up while Miss Hufnagel was giving a math lesson. My vision was blurry, and my desk was all damp from where I had been breathing on it. I must have woken up with a snort or something, because all the other kids started laughing.

"Back to the Land of the Living, Howie?" Miss Hufnagel said, and everybody laughed even harder. It was really embarrassing.

I figured that Miss Hufnagel must have called my parents to tell them about this incident. They were so worked up about the baby that I doubt they would have noticed how tired I was on their own.

"I've had a cold," I told them. "But I'm mostly better now." I did not, in fact, have a cold—but it was true that I was mostly better. You see, Casey Robinson was worried that her sleeping habits were going to hurt her schoolwork, so she decided she only wanted to use the portal on weekends and free afternoons. Kevin Bugg couldn't have cared less about his schoolwork, and things might have continued as usual with him. But *Mr.* Bugg had grown suspicious about our midnight journeys to Star Systems. He had come across crumbled bits of dirt on the floor in the shape of shoeprints, and one morning he had found the change cabinet of his G-Man and the Thing machine open, with the master key dangling from the lock. He suspected that a group of teenagers was breaking into the arcade at night to play the games, and he was planning to have security cameras installed. So that put an end to our late night trips to Star Systems.

The baby hadn't been born yet, but I knew that it wouldn't be long. Mom was only two weeks from her due date, and it looked like she was hiding a beach ball under her shirt. And still my parents had not agreed on a name. They wanted to make sure that the name would suit the child (or vice versa) and that it would not sound too bad with Quackenbush, which wasn't easy. My Aunt Margie ate dinner with us one night and told us that in certain tribal cultures the women only name their babies during those few seconds after they have gone to bed, when they are just beginning to drift off to sleep: they believe that this is when the spirits speak to them, and it's the only time they can be sure they won't choose the wrong name. When Aunt Margie was not around, though, our dinner conversations were a lot like our breakfast conversations. Lately, Mom and Dad had been considering what they called "gender-neutral" names, which meant names that could be used for either boys or girls. They had been reading about these names in Mom's *3,500 Names for Baby* book:

MOM (*opening the Señor Taco bag*): So far my favorite one on the list is Parker. "Of the park," it means.

DAD: Not bad, not bad. (*squirting hot sauce onto his taco*) But what else do we have?

MOM (*taking a bite of her chicken and avocado burrito*): Let's see. There's Kelly, Jordan, Drew, Casey . . .

HOWIE (*blushes senselessly*)

MOM: . . . Sandy, Winifred—I don't really like that one—Madison, Morgan, Hillary . . .

DAD (*pretending to choke on his food*): We can't name a boy *Hillary*. He'll get the snot beaten out of him at school.

81

MOM (*thinking for a moment*): That's not true. There was a boy in my class named Hillary when I was a little girl. I even dated him when I got older. He was one of the most popular boys in school. (*nodding in agreement with herself*) Yes, boys can certainly be named Hillary.

DAD (*trying not to smile*): Well, then, how about Pearl? If boys can be named Hillary, then boys can be named Pearl.

MOM: You've never known any boys named *Pearl*.

DAD: Sure I have. Pearl Johnson was one of my best friends when I was a kid. Ah, good old Pearl Johnson. The hours we spent playing with our toy soldiers and becoming young men together. You know, Pearl had a brother named Wanda—did I ever tell you about Wanda? A regular bulldozer of a guy, Wanda was. Their sister Hank, on the other hand—now *there* was a looker. . . .

It's no wonder I got stuck with Howie.

The next few days of school were pretty good. We had a social studies test and a health test, and we also had a spelling quiz. I made an A– on the social studies test, a B + on the health test, and an A+ on the spelling quiz. (I had been getting A+'s on all my spelling quizzes, in fact, ever since I had gotten the *Secret Guide to North Mellwood* and started spending so much time looking through my dad's dictionaries.) The weather had not warmed up enough for the snow to disappear, but we were still able to play soccer during recess. A truck had come to school one day and scraped the parking lot clean. Once, when I was playing goalie, I blocked a shot that went wobbling through the air behind me and landed chunk in the middle of one of the snowbanks. I started to run after the ball, but Mike Channering was standing right there talking to his friends. He plowed through the snow, fished the soccer ball out, and carried it back over to me. "Here you go, Quackenbush," he said. (He got my name right!) Then he walked back over to join his friends, his hands deep in his pockets.

Kevin Bugg, who was playing one of my blockers, looked at me curiously. "I thought Mike Channering hated your guts," he said.

I shrugged my shoulders. "I patched things up with him"

It was true that Mike Channering wasn't bullying me anymore—now he mostly just ignored me, which was much better. I kept waiting for him to ask me more questions about the *Secret Guide to North Mellwood*, like whether he could borrow it, or if the statue of Larry Boone always took you directly to the back of the Q*Bert machine, or how I had been able to leave a letter for him on his pillow. He never did, though. Maybe he figured it all out for himself, or maybe he just wasn't curious. I didn't care. I was just happy that I could walk through school every day without finding gum in my hair.

On Thursday, during our science lesson, our next shipment of books from *The Kids' Club Book Service Newsletter* arrived. Mr. Haddadi was back. He handed the big brown box with the red tape around the seams to Miss Hufnagel, bowing deeply to her and making a check mark on the metal clipboard he carried around with him. "Hello, Miss Hufnagel," he said. "Hello, precious little children." Then he smiled at us and left.

Miss Hufnagel handed the books out about thirty minutes before the end of school.

"I ordered *Matilda*, *Bunnicula*, and *The Jump Book*," said Jen Bertram as we were gathering around Miss Hufnagel's desk. "What did you order?"

"I ordered *A Wrinkle in Time*, *The Round and the Furry*, and *101 Pickle Jokes*," I said.

Jen Bertram grimaced. "I thought you ordered *101 Pickle Jokes* last time."

"I did," I said. She rolled her eyes at me. "Well," I told her, "it was a really good book."

Miss Hufnagel managed to get through every single kid—from Lionel Beef all the way down to Jim Zug—before the final bell rang. She told us that we could spend the last few minutes of class talking quietly, so long as our voices did not rise above a whisper. I flipped through the books I had ordered. There on my desk were *A Wrinkle in Time* and *The Round and the Furry*, exactly as they had looked in the catalog. But when I came to the last book, at the bottom of the stack, I felt a surge of excitement in my chest. Once again, the last book on my desk was not *101 Pickle Jokes*. It was not exactly the *Secret Guide to North Mellwood*, either. It was something called the *Secret Guide to North Mellwood: An Addendum*. I hunched over my desk so that nobody would see what I was doing and flipped open the book's cover. Inside, there was what appeared to be another map, only this one was printed on a sheet of transparent plastic instead of on regular paper. The map was too big for me to unfold in class without drawing attention to myself, so I decided to wait until I got home to look at it.

I motioned to Kevin Bugg, and he turned around in his seat. "Did you get the *Secret Guide*?" I whispered.

He looked absolutely miserable. "No," he said.

"Then you got *101 Pickle Jokes*?!" I whispered.

"No," he said again.

Now I was confused. "Then what did you get?"

He showed me the cover of his book. It had a picture of a man in a chef's hat holding a big purple onion. It was called *Great Onion Recipes for the Beginning Cook*. "My life sucks," said Kevin Bugg.

That afternoon, when I got home, I carefully investigated the *Secret Guide to North Mellwood: An Addendum*, unfolding it and spreading it out on my bedroom floor. It was roughly as large as the original map of North Mellwood, but it was made of stiff, transparent plastic. Also, it was mostly blank. There were no roads on it, for instance, no parks or lakes or railroad lines, and only a few dozen buildings which appeared to be floating in empty space. The buildings were marked by dotted black lines that were hard to see against my bedroom carpet at first, but their true names were printed on top of them in sharp black letters. I had no idea where any of the buildings were, though, and without any familiar landmarks to look at I had no way of finding out. Then it hit me: what if I placed *this* map on top of the other one? I took the *Secret Guide to North Mellwood* out of the drawer in my desk, which is where I had been keeping it, and opened it up on my bedroom floor. Then I spread the *Secret Guide to North Mellwood: An Addendum* out on top of it. The markings on the new map were much easier to see now, and I shifted it around until I had squared the corners. It fit perfectly!

The maps were definitely meant to go together—I was sure of that—but I was still confused by them. All of the new buildings, if that's what they were, were in strange places. They were directly on top of *old* buildings, or in the middle of the street, or hidden in the rock quarries south of town. One was even located right in the center of the Mellwood reservoir. Also, some of them were in places I passed by every single day on the way to school, and I was positive I hadn't seen any new buildings in those places. It didn't make any sense to me.

I heard Mom and Dad pulling into the driveway. I refolded the maps and zipped them into the inside pocket of my backpack just as the front door opened. "We're home, Howie," my dad called.

Tomorrow, I decided, I would have to see what I could learn.

Chapter 13

The next day, when I got to school, a kid I didn't know, some second-grader with curly yellow hair, came up to me and asked, "Have you smelled the big smell?"

"What are you talking about?" I said.

He looked really excited. "You *have* to smell the big smell," he said. Then he saw someone else stepping down from the bus and ran off to ask that kid if he had smelled the big smell. I assumed the kid was crazy and went inside.

All around me, in the hallway, kids were walking up to other kids and saying, "Have you smelled the big smell? Have you smelled the big smell? Have you smelled the big smell?" Some of the kids said they had smelled the big smell, and some of them said they hadn't. The ones who had said things like, "Where do you think it came from?" and "I've never smelled anything like it before." The ones who hadn't said exactly what I had said: "What on earth are you talking about?"

I had no idea what was going on. When I got to my classroom, I put my books away and took a seat at my desk. I tore the corner off a sheet of notebook paper and wadded it into a little white pellet. Then I threw the pellet at Kevin Bugg to get his attention. "What's this everybody is saying about the big smell?" I asked him.

He shook his head and made a bewildered shape with his eyebrows. "I'm clueless."

I turned to Casey Robinson and asked her the same question.

"Haven't you heard?" she said. She gave a funny little smile.

"I haven't heard," I said. "Hey, I wonder if—" but at just that moment the bell rang.

The sound of footsteps grew louder outside as all the kids rushed into their classrooms, and a few seconds later the doors shut one by one down the hallway. Miss Hufnagel paced back and forth by the chalk board while she took the morning roll ("Ha Nguyen, Sam Purcell, Howie Quackenbush, Casey Robinson . . ."). Usually, she sat at her desk while she took roll. When she was finished, she stood at the door putting her coat and mittens on. She snapped the buttons shut on the front of her coat, pulled the mittens tight between her thumbs and forefingers, yanked the laces at the neck of her coat and drew the collar together. Then she looked up at us. "Well, what are you waiting for, kids?" she said. "Get dressed."

We all got dressed and lined up at the front of the classroom. "Okay," Miss Hufnagel said. "Ordinarily we would begin the day with our English lesson. But today we have something else to take care of first. Right now," she said, "we're going to smell the big smell."

We followed Miss Hufnagel outside, through the snow, which was beginning to melt again, and across the courtyard of the school. We were about halfway to the statue of Larry Boone when the smell finally hit me. It was an odor of rotten eggs, and the closer we got to the statue, the stronger it became. By the time we reached the statue itself, the smell was almost overpowering. My eyes began to water, and a few of the other kids staggered backward. I knew exactly where the smell came from. So did Kevin Bugg. So did Casey Robinson. The quick stink I had noticed whenever I used the portal had somehow gotten out of control and formed this terrible cloud around Larry Boone. Miss Hufnagel covered her mouth and made a motion with her free hand to call us back inside. She was holding her breath, and her cheeks were puffed out like balloons.

When we got back to the classroom, we were all breathing really hard, as if we had just finished running a race. Ha Nguyen raised his hand to ask Miss Hufnagel a question. "What *was* that?"

"We're not quite sure," Miss Hufnagel answered.

Nina Fitzsimmons raised her hand, too. "It smells

like a dead body," she said.

"It does smell awful, Nina," said Miss Hufnagel, "but I don't think it's a dead body."

"Maybe it's a skunk," Melissa McGee said. "My brother shoots skunks sometimes, and that's what they smell like."

"It might be a skunk," said Miss Hufnagel, "but the principal doesn't think so, and neither do I. Our best guess is that a sewage pipe has burst beneath the statue. We've hired workers to begin digging up the ground, and they'll be here for the next several days. I want you children to stay away from that statue until we know what's going on, okay? You've smelled the big smell now, so there's no need to go exploring out there."

Later that morning, the workers arrived to begin their investigations. I saw them outside the window, measuring the base of the statue with a long silver tape measure. They wore orange hard hats and orange vests and the type of face masks you see doctors wearing on TV. They began to dig at the ground with spades and shovels, piling the dirt off to the side. The ground was still frozen from all the cold weather, and I could see that it was hard work. After a while, they rested. Then they set up a barrier of wooden trestles around the statue, fifteen or twenty of them, in a big circle. They strung yellow DO NOT CROSS streamers from trestle to trestle to seal all the gaps. By the time school let out, the workers had dug up to their waists on all sides of the statue. I walked by on my way to the bus and saw them carving the dirt away from a few shiny metal pipes that ran beneath the ground. The smell was still as strong as before.

"This is terrible," I said to Casey Robinson as I sat beside her on the bus.

"What, the smell?" she said.

"Well . . . I guess the smell is pretty terrible," I said. "But I meant all the construction. I was hoping to use the portal this afternoon."

"What for?" She was rubbing a strawberry-flavored lip balm over her lips.

"I'm not sure yet," I said, "but I'll tell you as soon as I know." My shoulders gave a shiver of delight as I answered her. This keeping secrets—it was sort of fun.

Casey sighed through her nose. "I hate it when you do that. Why can't you just tell me?"

"Because I don't really know yet," I said. I thought about it for a second. I always hated it when people kept secrets from me. And maybe Casey Robinson could help me come up with a solution. "Okay. Yesterday, instead of *101 Pickle Jokes*, I got another map—a new one. It fits together with the map I already had, but I can't tell where any of the buildings are supposed to be." I pulled the *Secret Guide to North Mellwood: An Addendum* out of my backpack and opened the book just a little bit to show her a corner of the map. "See," I said, "you place this map on top of the other one, and it shows you where the new buildings are. The problem is that all the new buildings are in strange places—one of them is even in the middle of the Mellwood reservoir. I can't figure it out."

"The map is transparent, right?" Casey Robinson said. "Have you thought about flipping it over? Maybe you're looking at the wrong side."

"I tried that," I said, "but if you turn it upside down, all the true names come out backward. That can't be right. I was planning to use the statue of Larry Boone to investigate, but with all those workmen out there, who knows when I'll be able to do that?"

Casey Robinson capped her lip balm and slipped it back into her pocket. "What about using one of the other portals? Have you thought about that?"

"I'd love to, but I don't know where any of them are."

"Well," she said. "It looks like you're stuck. I'll let you know if I think of anything."

I was grumpy for the rest of the afternoon. I was upset because the statue of Larry Boone had come to seem like it belonged to me, and now there were men in hard hats digging all around it. It occurred to me suddenly that they might even uproot the statue and take it away. I didn't know what I would do if that happened. Thinking about it, I felt even worse than I had before. Even Rhubarb seemed to notice. I was lying on the carpet watching TV, and she walked over and stepped onto my chest. She turned around a few times as if she was about to curl up and go to sleep, but then she looked me in the eye. She swung to the floor and wandered off into the kitchen.

That night I slept at my Aunt Margie's house. This was something I did every three months or so, and it was always a treat. Usually the two of us rented movies and ate popcorn in the living room, and then stayed up talking until we were too tired to talk anymore. For breakfast we always ordered doughnuts from one of the Doughnut Brothers doughnut shops. My dad dropped me off at Aunt Margie's around six o'clock that night. "You'll give us a call if it's baby time, won't you?" Aunt Margie said when she met him at the car.

"Of course," he said. It was only one week until my mom's due date, and the doctor had told her to be ready at any moment. She was spending most of her time lately propped up in bed reading magazines and eating her meals off a tray. "I want you and Howie to be there in the waiting room when the time comes," my father said.

He gave Aunt Margie a couple of dollars for the movies and drove off.

The first movie we rented that night was called *The All-Girl Football Team*. It was my choice. It was about a town where all the guys on the football team get sick with the flu, so the girls on the cheerleading squad have to substitute for them during the big game. It was a pretty funny movie, but I was in such a bad mood that I don't think I laughed even once. We never watched the second movie at all. This is because Aunt Margie noticed the sour mood I was in, and asked me what was wrong.

"You wouldn't understand," I said.

She sat back in her chair, folding her arms across her lap. "Try me."

"Okay," I said. "But I'm warning you, you're not going

to believe me." I told Aunt Margie about both the *Secret Guide to North Mellwood* and the *Secret Guide to North Mellwood: An Addendum*. I told her about the five secret portals, and the true names, and the statue of Larry Boone, and the big smell. "And now that the workmen are out there, I won't be able to get to the statue for who knows how long," I finished. "It's all just a big mess."

The whole time I was telling my story, I could see Aunt Margie squirming around in her chair, and biting her lip, and trying to keep the laughter from sneaking into the corners of her mouth. By the time I had finished, she just couldn't help herself. She exploded. She clutched her stomach and doubled over, and her face turned a bright glossy red, like a tomato. I had never seen her laugh so hard in all my life.

My feelings were a little bit hurt. "I don't see what's so funny," I told her.

"I'm sorry, I'm sorry," Aunt Margie said. The words were coming out between giant bursts of laughter. After a while, she managed to calm down. "Come with me," she said. She took my hand and led me down the hallway. Every few seconds she would start laughing again, and I would feel it shuddering through my palms. She took me into the White Room, the perfectly empty space in the center of her house where she liked to meditate and exercise. There was a faint smell of incense in the air, and I could hear the refrigerator humming in the real kitchen. She turned the ceiling light on, and the walls glowed a brilliant white.

94

"I wish you had told me what your problem was sooner," Aunt Margie said, dropping my hand. She began to giggle again, but then stopped herself. She knocked three times on the blank white wall at the back of the room. "Floccinaucinihilipilification," she said. And she disappeared.

Chapter 14

There were five portals pictured in the *Secret Guide to North Mellwood*—the statue of Larry Boone, the two warehouses, the hollowed-out tree, and the blank white wall in somebody's house. The blank white wall, it turned out, was right in front of me. And the somebody whose house it was in was my Aunt Margie.

I was so exhilarated when she returned that I could feel my heart beating inside my chest in great skips and leaps. I could barely speak. "But how . . . When did you . . . I can't . . ."

She smiled. She lit a stick of cinnamon incense with a match and placed it in an incense holder on the floor. The orange ember began to travel down the length of the stick, giving off a pleasant-smelling smoke that curled through the air. "I've known about the portals since

I was, oh, fourteen or fifteen years old. It took me a few years to find all five of them, though. The easiest was the statue of Larry Boone. You know where that is, of course, and now you know where the blank white wall is. The hollowed-out oak tree is at the edge of a clearing behind McSalty's Pizza Parlor. And the two warehouses are located in the industrial section of town—though they're right across the street from each other, so one of them is pretty useless."

I wanted to ask Aunt Margie whether I could have permission to use the portal in her White Room every once in a while, but I couldn't find a moment to interrupt her. She was on a roll.

"I suppose you're wondering how I came to have a portal in my very own home. Well, why do you think I bought this house to begin with? The man who was living here before me had absolutely no idea there was a portal in his study. In fact, he had the whole wall covered with two huge maps of the moon. He was an amateur astronomer, and his life revolved around the telescopes he owned. When I first came here, there were telescopes poking out from every window in the house—they made the place look like some kind of porcupine. The man who was living here said that North Mellwood was getting so bright that he couldn't see the stars properly anymore, so he decided to move to the country. I snapped the house right up. I don't use the portal so often these days—only when I'm really in a hurry. When you get older, you like a slower pace. But I'm excited about the *Addendum*. I've never seen it before, though I've got a copy of the *Guide* around here somewhere. I never did find out who sent it to me. It just showed up in the mailbox one day. You'll have to let me know what—" She stopped herself suddenly, touching a hand to her mouth. "You know, I've been wanting to talk about this for so long that it's all come out in a blather. I'm sorry about that."

"Aunt Margie," I asked, "do you think it would be okay if . . . ?"

I let my voice trail off, but she understood. "You can use the portal whenever you want to, Howie. But you have to promise me one thing: when you've finished for the day, you'll light a stick of incense. I keep a jar of them in the hall closet, along with an incense holder. They help to get rid of that rotten egg smell."

Chapter 15

It was Saturday morning—a clear, bright morning with the sound of melting snow trickling through the gutters. Aunt Margie took me to eat our usual breakfast at the Doughnut Brothers doughnut shop. She ate two plain cake doughnuts and drank a cup of hazelnut coffee. I ate a cherry-filled doughnut and a custard-filled doughnut and drank a carton of whole milk. Many people I know don't like filled doughnuts because of the way the breaded part grows thin in the middle and leaves you with a mouthful of jam. I'm just the opposite. I don't mind the jam one bit, but I don't like the way the glaze on the outside of regular doughnuts sticks to your fingers and makes you have to lick them clean. The Doughnut Brothers don't put any glaze at all on the outside of their filled doughnuts. This is what makes them so good.

While we ate, Aunt Margie told me about her first experience with the *Secret Guide to North Mellwood*. She said that transporting from place to place when she was fourteen or fifteen years old made her see the town in a whole new way. Everything seemed to be connected by these floating invisible strings that she never knew were there, and she began to imagine them crisscrossing through the air in the shape of stars and webs and flowers. It was beautiful, she said. She was in the ninth grade at the time, and she was taking a class in school called Career Orientation. The class was supposed to help her figure out what she should be when she grew up, but all the tests told her that she should either manage a bowling alley or work in a bowling pin factory or design new kinds of bowling balls. "I hated bowling, though," she said. "I didn't know what to do. In some funny way, it was the *Secret Guide* that first made me want to become an artist."

After breakfast, I walked to Casey Robinson's house. I didn't use the portal to get there because it was Saturday morning and I knew that her parents would be home. I wanted to make a good impression, and I figured that suddenly appearing in their kitchen would not be the best way to do it. Also, Casey Robinson lives only a few blocks from my Aunt Margie, so I knew that it wouldn't take me long to walk there. There were patches of brown slush on the sidewalks, but the concrete wasn't dangerous or slippery—it was mostly just wet from the melting snow. All around me, small rivers of water were flowing into the street. The sun was reflecting from every surface.

I had never met Casey Robinson's mother before, but when she answered the door, she seemed to know who I was right away. She invited me in and led me to a seat in the living room. "Casey!" she called. "Howie Quackenbush is here!" Casey came running down the hall from her bedroom. She must have just washed her hair because it was darker than its usual color.

"I came to see if you'd like to go out for a while," I said. I nodded to her—a signal that I had something private to say.

"Can I, Mom?" she asked.

Mrs. Robinson was paging through a magazine. "As long as you're back this afternoon, honey."

We walked back to my Aunt Margie's house together. Casey Robinson deliberately left a footprint in the center of each slush pile, spraying slush across the sidewalk. By the time we had gone a block, the cuffs of my pants were covered with it. I told her all about the portal in the White Room, and that I wanted her and Kevin Bugg to help me explore the buildings that were in the *Secret Guide to North Mellwood: An Addendum*. "So the portal was in your aunt's house all along?" she asked.

"Looks like it," I said.

"Well, I guess you solved your problem," she said.

"Looks like it," I said again.

I left Casey Robinson to talk with Aunt Margie while I went to get Kevin Bugg. He lives a little bit farther away from Aunt Margie than Casey does, so I used the portal to get to his house. I wasn't worried about scaring his mother because I knew that I would land in the driveway.

Kevin Bugg smelled like onions.

When the two of us got back, Casey and Aunt Margie were painting one of her Eskimo sculptures together. She has fifty or sixty of these sculptures, all identical, which sit on a set of shelves on either side of her front hall. The Eskimo sculptures are bulky wooden figures, about the size of toasters. They wear pale green anoraks and have arms you can rotate on pivots. Casey and Aunt Margie looked like they were having a great time, and part of me wished that I'd been able to stay behind to hear what they'd said to each other.

"We were just talking about what you were like when you were a little boy," Aunt Margie said. Casey Robinson looked at her, and they both giggled. They wouldn't tell me anything more. Secrets.

I asked Aunt Margie to call my parents and tell them I wouldn't be home until late that afternoon. Then Casey Robinson, Kevin Bugg, and I went together into the White Room. I unfolded the map to North Mellwood, and the addendum to the map, and spread them out together on the floor. "So where do you want to go first?" I asked. We all looked at the two maps and at the dozen or so buildings marked by dotted black lines on the sheet of transparent plastic. "Let's try this one," said Kevin Bugg. He pointed to a building that seemed to be located in the middle of the street right outside Aunt Margie's front door. The true name printed there was OSTIUM. "That way if we don't like what we find, or if the true name doesn't work to bring us back home, we can run straight back inside."

"I don't know," Casey Robinson said. "It doesn't seem like a good idea to transport ourselves right into the middle of traffic."

Aunt Margie lives on a pretty quiet street—with lots of bicycles and pedestrians and trees in wooden barrels—so I wasn't particularly worried about the traffic. But I could see that Casey had a point. "It's up to you," I said. "If you want to try it, we will. Otherwise, we'll pick someplace else."

She thought about it for a minute. "Well . . . okay. I guess I'm up for it."

We gathered together by the blank white wall at the back of the room. I knocked on it three times. "All right," I said. "Grab hold of me." Kevin Bugg took my left arm, and Casey Robinson took my right. "Ostium," I said, and we found ourselves standing in a small, square room lit by a fluorescent light. Against the walls, all four of them, was a pattern of black lines with tiny red lights traveling along them. These lights moved in all directions. At first, they reminded me of ants running from a crumbled anthill along a hundred different paths, but the more I looked at them, the more confusing they became. In some places there were a lot of the tiny red lights, and in some places there were hardly any. Occasionally, a group of them would stand still for a minute or two before starting up again. I couldn't figure out why they were moving all over the place like that. As we were examining the lights, something rumbled across the roof of the room we were in,

103

causing the fluorescent light to tremble on the ceiling. My mom and dad always complain about the noise I make when I throw my soccer ball onto the roof. At first I thought that that was the noise I was listening to—some kid with a soccer ball. But then it happened again, and I realized that it was far too loud.

Casey Robinson was staring intently at one particular section of the wall. "I think I've figured it out," she said. "Watch. The ceiling is going to shake again on the count of . . . one, two, three—" The ceiling shook, and the light trembled.

"How did you figure that out?" said Kevin Bugg.

Casey Robinson pointed to a spot on one of the lines she was watching. "We're right here," she said. "The lines are the streets of North Mellwood. And the little red lights must be cars and trucks." Suddenly the pattern on the wall made sense to me. It *was* North Mellwood, only without the buildings and parks and streams I was used to seeing on the map. Some of the streets were busier than others. Some started out small and quiet and then joined up with other streets and turned into wide boulevards. The tiny red lights that paused at the intersections were waiting together at stop lights, and the ones that disappeared completely were pulling off the road and parking in their garages. The ceiling shook again as another red light passed beneath the tip of Casey's finger. We were underground.

"I don't see a door, do you?" said Kevin Bugg, looking around. "There's no door to this room."

He was right. It looked like the only way to get in or out was by way of the portal. It occurred to me that if I wanted to get rid of somebody, it would be the easiest thing in the world to do: just transport them here, let go of them, and transport back to the White Room without them.

The lights on the wall were interesting to look at for a while. Once we knew they were cars and trucks, they were surprisingly beautiful. We got bored with them pretty quickly, though. "This room doesn't seem very useful," I said. "I mean, maybe if you're trying to figure out which roads to avoid in the snow, or if you need to know where an accident is, but who needs to know things like that?"

"It reminds me of a science experiment," Casey Robinson said. "All the curving lines and moving lights."

Kevin Bugg yawned. "Let's go back," he said.

I agreed. Casey Robinson and Kevin Bugg took hold of me and I said "Ostium." We were standing in the White Room again.

Over the next hour or two, we transported to a few more of the rooms on the *Addendum to North Mellwood*. They were all pretty much like the first one—interesting, but in a limited sort of way, like a puzzle that you want to toss in your closet as soon as you've finished solving it. We found one room that we called the Monkey Room: in this room there were dozens of small monkeys with gray ruffs of hair around their faces. It was a big room, the size of a gymnasium, with lots of ropes and poles and ladders to climb, and the monkeys were swinging all over the place.

They gathered around us as soon as we appeared and beckoned us to follow them over to the far side of the room, where there was a toggle switch placed high on the wall. The toggle switch was too high for them to reach. I can't explain how I knew what they wanted me to do, but I did. I pulled the switch and a hatch opened in the wall. Out tumbled a big cardboard box with red tape around the seams. The monkeys tore the box apart. They found another box inside of it. They tore *that* box apart and found yet another box. They tore the last box apart and found a bunch of bananas. They ate the bananas.

We found another room which we called the Room of Failed Inventions. The Room of Failed Inventions had dozens of pedestals standing across the floor. Every pedestal had a glass box on top of it, and inside every glass box was a different invention. The boxes were easy to open, and Casey and Kevin and I examined a few of them. Inside one box, for instance, was a gold ring with a white tag that read RING OF INVISIBILITY on it. This sounded really exciting, but when I put the ring on, it only made my fingernails disappear—nothing else. Making your fingernails disappear is a pretty neat trick, I guess, but I couldn't think of any real practical use for it, so I put the ring back in the box. All of the inventions were like that— cool for about ten seconds and then kind of ridiculous. There was a pair of glasses that made everything look upside down and far away, and a set of car keys that bounced around like a frog so that we couldn't catch them. There was a miniature air hockey table that sucked air in instead of blowing air out, so that when we set the hockey puck on top of it, it just sort of stuck there. We couldn't get it to move until we turned the machine off. And there was a lump of pinkish clay as heavy and hard as a rock that made a dent in the floor when we dropped it. The white tag on the clay read SERIOUS PUTTY.

We found another room that we called the Room of Lost Pets. This room was filled with a thick white fog. We could hardly see each other's faces. We kept stumbling into cats and dogs whose collars were missing their nametags. The animals meowed and barked each time our legs brushed against them, but they went quiet whenever we picked them up to examine them. We also found a few lizards and birds and hamsters and such. I was surprised that so many animals could be in the same room without fighting all the time. Maybe that's why it was so cloudy in there—so they wouldn't tear each other to pieces. It was kind of sad to see all of the pets without their owners, and Casey wanted to take them back to North Mellwood with us, but I didn't see how we would ever be able to find their original homes, and I knew that our parents wouldn't let us keep them. At least mine wouldn't. The fog in the Room of Lost Pets made Kevin Bugg sneeze, so we ended up leaving after only a few minutes.

We found another room that was almost exactly like the first one we saw except that the tiny red lights were people instead of cars and trucks. The room would have been great if we had known who each of the lights was, but we didn't, and we couldn't see any way to figure it out.

"What about this room?" Kevin Bugg said when we had transported back to Aunt Margie's apartment. He was pointing to a room that was surrounding—or was underneath—the statue of Larry Boone at the elementary school. The true name printed there was EUHEMERISM.

"Don't forget I have to be home this afternoon," Casey Robinson said. "What time is it?"

I looked at my watch. "It's barely noon. We can go to this one last room and then call it quits for the day. How does that sound?" Kevin Bugg and Casey Robinson agreed to this plan. Before we left for the last room, we ate lunch. Aunt Margie had gone out for the afternoon, but she had left a tray of egg and mayonnaise sandwiches on the floor of the White Room for us. There was a note on top of the sandwiches:

Hope you guys are having a good time. You'll have to tell me all about it later. Howie, your mom and dad will be expecting to see you home around five this evening. Love, Aunt Margie. Oh, and don't forget the incense.

After we had finished eating, I folded up the two maps and slipped them into the big front pocket of my winter coat. They made a bulge there that I could feel against my stomach, and for a moment I thought about what it must feel like to be my mom, carrying ten pounds of baby around inside her. "Okay, are you ready?" I asked. Casey Robinson and Kevin Bugg said that they were. We returned the tray with the sandwich crumbs to the kitchen, and I left a note for Aunt Margie telling her that I would see her that afternoon if she was back—or, if she wasn't, I would see her in a few days.

I knocked three times on the wall of the White Room and joined hands with Kevin Bugg and Casey Robinson. "Euhemerism," I said. The room we landed in was dimly lit. The light came from a small brass lamp that was sitting on a polished wooden end table. I could see some sort of light fixture hanging from the ceiling as well, but it wasn't turned on. The carpet was dark and deep. I could feel how soft it was even through my shoes. There was a couch in the room, and a few armchairs, and a desk made of the same polished wood as the end table with the brass lamp.

There was also a person in the room. He was sitting on the couch rubbing lotion into the backs of his hands and staring up at us with his nut-colored eyes. He was wearing blue jeans and a sweater vest. He had an easy smile on his face. "Hello," he said. "I'm Larry Boone."

Chapter 16

We were shocked.

"Larry Boone, the Revolutionary War hero?" Kevin Bugg asked. "That Larry Boone?"

The man laughed, a warm, bright laugh. "Is that what they're saying about me now? No, I guess you could say I'm a builder—or maybe an inventor. I designed the elementary school, for instance, and the fire station on Park Street, and I've invented all sorts of things. But most of them don't work very well." He stood up and walked over to his desk. "Revolutionary War hero. Ha! I've got to write that down." He turned another lamp on, and then scribbled something onto a little yellow pad of paper. "Please," he said, without bothering to look up from his desk. "Go ahead and have a seat. I'll be with you in a minute."

Casey, Kevin, and I sat down in the armchairs beside the couch. We were all sitting very still and looking around nervously at each other. I could tell that we were thinking the same thing: that we should be ready to bolt from there at any second. After all, who knew who this guy really was? He said he was Larry Boone, and he looked like Larry Boone, but none of us thought he really was Larry Boone. We were wrong, but that's what we thought.

"Now then," Larry Boone said, returning to the couch. "You must be Howie Quackenbush, which would make this Kevin Bugg, and this Casey Robinson." He pointed to each of us in turn.

"How did you know our names?" said Casey Robinson.

"Oh, I know just about everything," Larry Boone said. "Didn't you wonder where the *Secret Guide to North Mellwood* came from? I've been watching the three of you very closely these past few weeks. By the way," he said to Casey Robinson, "strawberry really isn't your scent. You would do much better with vanilla."

I made a soft noise in my throat. "No offense, sir—" I said.

"Larry," said Larry Boone. "Please call me Larry."

"Well," I said, "that's what I wanted to talk to you about. You see, we're not really sure that you *are* Larry Boone. Again, no offense, but Larry Boone's been dead for more than two hundred years."

"Do I look dead to you?" he said, and he laughed. "Look, Howie—can I call you Howie?" I nodded. "Would it help if I showed you my Being License?" He pulled a laminated card from the pocket of his shirt and passed it around to us. On the top of the card were the words BEING LICENSE, and beneath them and to the right was a picture of Larry Boone. He was smiling in the picture with the same sunny smile he wore right now, and his hair was parted to the side with the same sharp white part. Beside the picture was his name—LARRY BOONE—as well as his signature and a list of statistics: height, weight, date of birth, things like that. There was even an expiration date listed, though it was years in the future and hadn't happened yet. I realized as I looked at it that he really was Larry Boone.

"Excuse me, Mr. Boone?" said Casey Robinson.

"Larry," said Larry Boone.

"Excuse me, Larry, but what's a Being License? I don't think any of us have ever heard of one before."

"Oh, everybody has a Being License," Larry Boone said. "Being is what makes the world go round, and you could hardly *be* without the proper authorization. You need the proper authorization to do almost anything nowadays. You, Howie, Kevin—and by the way, Kevin, the diet is working wonders for you—all three of you have Being Licenses. Otherwise you couldn't very well *be* here with me today, now could you? I just happen to carry my Being License around with me, and a good thing, too, considering the number of times I've been pulled over. I've gotten tickets for Being Too Fast, Reckless Being, Being While under the Influence . . . you name it, I've done

112

it. Everything except Being without a License, that is."
He flashed the laminated card at us and then slid it back
into his pocket. "You know, you would look so much more
dignified with your hair trimmed short at the sides,
Howie."

I noticed that Larry Boone had a lot of advice to give.
It seemed like he couldn't talk for more than ten seconds
without popping off another suggestion. "How did you
come to be living down here under the ground?" I asked. I
presumed that that was where we were—underneath the
statue.

Larry Boone gave a deep, satisfied breath and looked
around at the drawing room. "Well, the main thing is that
I like peace and quiet in my life, and this seemed the best
place to find it." Just then a noise of footsteps and clinking
metal came from above us: it was the workmen resuming
their afternoon digging. "Or it *was* the best place to find it
until yesterday." Larry Boone sighed. He went to the corner of the room, grabbed a broomstick, and pounded the
handle against the ceiling. "Pipe down!" he shouted. "Hey,
keep it quiet up there!" The noise suddenly fell off. I could
picture the workmen up above us removing their hard hats
to scratch their heads and look around at each other.

"I'm hoping that all the banging and scraping will stop
as soon as the smell goes away," said Larry Boone.

"That's what Miss Hufnagel told us would happen," I
said.

We talked for a long time. Larry Boone told us about
the history of North Mellwood and about his own life

under the ground. Half the time I couldn't tell whether he was being serious or putting us on. For instance, he told us that Mellwood meant "forest of the Mels," and that this area was once covered in woodland and inhabited by a tribe of people called the Melungeons, who went by the name "the Mels" for short. He told us that for many years there was a South Mellwood on the other side of the reservoir, but that it was destroyed long ago in a terrible haying accident. He said that it was nice living underground—that it was cool in the summer, warm in the winter—but that you had to be careful of moles and earthworms and burrowing owls, who would try to tunnel through your walls. He said that Casey Robinson and I made a nice couple. He said that he had designed the portals a long time ago and that he used the rooms underneath the city mostly for storage and observation—but not all of them. He said that he tried to feed the monkeys in the Monkey Room four or five times a day, but sometimes he only managed to make it down there once or twice. He said that the monkeys had learned how to make a ladder of their own bodies in order to pull the toggle switch on the wall, like the plastic monkeys in the game Barrel Full o'Monkeys, but that they were lazy and preferred for him to pull it for them. He said that you could tell when the sun was out and when the moon was out even when you were living underground by the motion of the various creatures in the soil. He told Kevin Bugg that he looked like a "hamster person," and that he should ask his mom to buy him one for a pet.

My attention wandered sometimes while Larry Boone was speaking. I couldn't help it. It wasn't that he wasn't interesting—but he simply had so *much* to say. I looked around the room while he was talking. I looked at the light reflecting from the brass lamp stand. I looked at Casey Robinson and Kevin Bugg. I looked at the paintings of North Mellwood covering the walls. I looked at the stacks of books in the corner, and the flattened cardboard boxes, and the rolls of bright red tape. They were the same kind of boxes I had seen in the Monkey Room, and the same kind that Mr. Haddadi delivered the books from *The Kids' Club Book Service Newsletter* in.

After a long time, Larry Boone stopped talking. It took me a few minutes to realize that he had stopped, since I had zoned out some time ago and was now staring at a blank space in the air. For the last hour or two, in fact, his voice had been just a quiet buzz in the center of my head. I wondered if this was what being hypnotized felt like.

The room was so quiet that it felt strange to speak. I cleared my throat. "All these books and boxes and rolls of red tape," I said. "They're from the Kids' Club Book Service, aren't they?"

"They're not just *from* the Kids' Club Book Service," Larry Boone said. "I *am* the Kids' Club Book Service."

"Then you really did send me the *Secret Guide to North Mellwood*. But why?"

Larry Boone gave me one of his smiles. "There's a room you're supposed to visit, Howie," he said. "I'm sure you'll figure it out."

I didn't know what to say to that. Before I could think of another question, Casey Robinson interrupted us. "I think it's about time for us to go, Mr. . . . er, Larry. We're supposed to be home for dinner before too long."

I looked at my watch. She was right. It was getting late.

"So you are, so you are," said Larry Boone. "You know, I have to tell you that I've enjoyed our conversation. I don't get too many visitors down here, and a person needs someone to talk to. You children feel free to come back any time."

"We will," I said.

My knees made a popping noise when I stood. The three of us walked across the room to the spot where we had landed and joined hands. "Good-bye, Larry," we said, and "See you soon," and "Good luck with the monkeys." Then I took a deep breath and said, "Euhemerism."

Nothing happened. I tried it again: "Euhemerism."

Still nothing.

I looked at my watch and saw that it was 4:30. We had been listening to Larry Boone for more than four hours, and the portal effect had worn off! I felt a sense of panic in my stomach, a blind, trembling feeling. I turned to Kevin Bugg and Casey Robinson. "We're stuck," I said.

I had no real reason to worry. Larry Boone was listening from his seat on the couch. "Oh dear," he said. "I forgot all about the time. Well, there's nothing else to do. I guess you'll just have to use the passageway."

"The passageway?" Casey Robinson said.

"Yes, yes," Larry Boone answered. He brushed his jeans off as if there were crumbs on them, though they were perfectly clean. "The passageway is right over here," he said. "Follow me."

He led us to a wall panel behind his desk. He opened a door there by pushing his fingers into a groove at the side and then sliding the whole panel into the wall. This left a space in the wall that was just large enough for us to climb through. "All you have to do is follow this passageway and it will take you straight to the center of town," Larry Boone said. "Oh, and Howie, don't forget: there's another room for you to visit soon."

I entered the passageway with Kevin Bugg and Casey Robinson, and Larry Boone slid the panel shut behind us. "Bye, now," he said, and then we couldn't see him anymore. The walls of the tunnel we were in were made entirely of dirt. There were wooden braces placed against the sides every few feet, and these braces were covered with a strange glowing mold that made it possible for us to see. White pipes ran along certain sections of the wall, half-concealed by the dirt. Every so often one of the pipes would stretch across the passageway, and we would have to duck our heads down in order to pass underneath. A few spots on the wall were practically boiling with earthworms, which made Casey Robinson jump and left me feeling a little sick myself. Eventually we reached the surface. The tunnel ended inside a hollowed-out oak tree behind McSalty's Pizza Parlor. The ice was still melting from the branches of the tree as we stepped out into the sun. This was, in fact, the very same hollowed-out oak tree that was pictured inside the *Secret Guide to North Mellwood*, but I was tired and it took me a few more days to figure that out, so we ended up walking home instead of transporting.

We reached Kevin Bugg's house first, and then Casey Robinson and I walked the few blocks back to hers. Before I left her, the most wonderful thing happened: she kissed me. We were standing on her front porch, and she was just about to go inside when she leaned forward and kissed me on the lips. It was over almost before I knew what was happening. Being kissed by Casey Robinson didn't really feel too much different from being tapped on the lips by somebody's finger, but I felt my face growing hot anyway. I could tell by the way Casey laughed that I was turning beet red, which is something that happens to me when I get embarrassed. For a moment I couldn't say anything. Then, when I finally did speak, all I managed to say was, "Thanks"—which, when I thought about it later that night, made me blush even more. Casey Robinson squeezed my hand and went inside, and I was so excited that I decided to run the rest of the way home. After a few blocks, though, I was out of breath and had to catch the bus. My parents were waiting for me in the kitchen when I got home, and dinner was already on the table.

Chapter 17

It was Monday afternoon before I could follow Larry Boone's advice and visit the next room on the map. This was because on Sunday morning, while I was reading the comics section of the newspaper, my mom told us that she had gone into labor. First she was just washing her face in the bathroom, and then all of a sudden she was holding her stomach and saying, "I think it's time." We threw her toothbrush and her makeup bag and a change of clothes into the suitcase, and we rushed her to the hospital. In the car, after about five minutes or so, she gave this cry of surprise and then started panting with a "hoo-hoo-hoo" sound. She sounded like a train that was chugging real hard in order to get started down the tracks. We parked right by the entrance to the hospital. My dad helped her walk inside. I carried the suitcase.

When we got inside, a nurse took my mom and dad to the delivery room. Another nurse came up to me and placed her hand on my head. She said, "Howie, why don't I take you to the waiting room? There are some other kids there, and you can watch TV or read a magazine or do whatever you want while you wait." I wasn't surprised that the nurse knew my name. Everybody knew who my mom was because she worked at the hospital, and I guess she had shown them pictures of me or something.

I wished that I could be in the delivery room. The waiting room was boring. All of the magazines were about fishing or home decorating or movie stars that I had never heard of. A little kid was running all over the place chasing another little kid, and one or the other of them kept bumping into me. Their dad (at least I assumed he was their dad) was blowing his nose into a handkerchief, and every few seconds or so he halfheartedly told the kids to sit down and be quiet, but it had no effect. There was a TV in the room, but it was playing one of those Sunday morning church programs. The TV was placed high against the ceiling on one of those metal arms, and I couldn't reach it to change the station. I felt like one of the monkeys in the Monkey Room.

I sat around in the waiting room for about an hour and a half before the nurse came to get me. She took me to my parents, who were already dressed and ready to go back home. I expected to see a new baby in my mom's arms, but it turned out that she was still pregnant. "False alarm, Howie," my dad said. "We'll try again in a couple of days."

My mom's cheeks were shining with tears. I could see that she had been crying, but I didn't know why. After all, there was nothing wrong with the baby—it just wasn't ready to be born yet. And while my mom had been in pain a few hours earlier, she looked okay now. Maybe she didn't know why she had been crying either.

When we got home, she went straight up to her bedroom and slept the rest of the day. My dad told me that we should be extra quiet so that we wouldn't wake her. He explained to me that there was something called false labor. It was when the body of a pregnant woman told her that she was ready to have her baby before she actually was. This was what had happened to my mom and what had left her so tired.

The next morning she seemed much better. I said good-bye to her in her bedroom before I caught the bus to school. She was lying with her head propped up against the headboard, reading a book. "I was worried about you, you know," I said.

She looked at me. "I know," she said. She gave a slow, sweet smile. "Thanks, honey."

At school that day, we watched a filmstrip about DNA. It was called *DNA: The Bonds of Life*, and it was hosted by a man in a wheelchair who talked about how every person in the world is like a grain of snow: "Cold and flaky," he said, and then he laughed through his voice box. "But seriously folks—we are all, every one of us, precious and unique, and like a grain of snow we're also very fragile." Miss Hufnagel gave us a worksheet that afternoon on multiplying and dividing fractions, which is not as easy as it sounds. We also talked about the people and customs of the country of Brazil, and about the difference between fact and opinion. At the end of Question and Answer Time, I told the story of my trip to the hospital with my mom and dad. Everybody wanted to know whether the baby was going to be a boy or a girl, and I told them that my parents were keeping it a surprise. The workmen were still milling around by the statue of Larry Boone, and I could see them through the window while I sat at my desk.

After school, I got off the bus with Melissa McGee and Lionel Beef at the stop right down the street from my Aunt Margie's house. She wasn't home, but I knew she kept her spare key hidden beneath one of the potted plants on her front porch. I let myself inside. "Hello?" I shouted. Nobody answered. I walked past the twin shelves of Eskimos, past the living room, the real kitchen and the fake kitchen, and into the White Room at the center of the house.

Larry Boone had told me that there was "another room for me to visit soon," but he didn't tell me which room he meant. I unfolded the *Secret Guide to North Mellwood* and the *Secret Guide to North Mellwood: An Addendum* and spread them out together on the floor. There were still a dozen or so buildings on the *Addendum* that I hadn't been to yet. I looked them over to see which one I should try first. There was one in the rock quarries south of town with the true name GOMBROON. There was one on top of the Redwing Bait and Tackle Shop with the true name

TORFLE. There was one in the center of the Mellwood reservoir with the true name MULTIPARITY. There were others dotted all over the map. I saw no way to decide between them.

Eventually, out of sheer curiosity, I chose the room in the center of the Mellwood reservoir. I wanted to see what a room under water would look like. Would it be dark and narrow, like a submarine? Would it be like the underwater cities I had seen in comic books, bubbles of glass with people walking around inside them? Or would it be just a hollow place in the water itself, without walls of any kind? I was a little bit frightened of drowning down there, but I had managed to transport beneath the street without getting hit by a car, so I figured I would be all right. I knocked three times on the wall at the back of the room, held my breath (just in case), and said "Multiparity."

I was standing in front of a wide yellow door. There was an umbrella stand by the door with six or seven busted umbrellas inside it. There was also a welcome mat for you to wipe your feet on. I figured that I must be inside the Mellwood reservoir, or just beneath it, since I could hear the sloshing sounds of water coming from nearby. Every so often something would slap against the ceiling of the hall—a fish, I guessed. From inside the yellow door I could hear gurgling noises and sucking noises and what sounded like quiet conversation. There was a sign above the door that said HALL OF BABIES.

I opened the door and was greeted by the strangest sight I have ever seen. There were twenty or thirty babies in the room, all of them naked. They were sitting in small leather armchairs or padded love seats, and they looked perfectly comfortable. Some of the babies were really tiny, about the size of my thumb, and looked a little bit like fish. But most of the babies were just regular babies, about the size of footballs, and looked exactly like you would expect them to look—like miniature people. Their heads lolled to the side, and every so often one of them would give a kick into the air. A few of the babies were drooling or sucking on their thumbs. Each of them had a long, thick umbilical cord stretching away from their belly button, and these cords disappeared into various small holes in the wall. I got the impression that the babies had been talking comfortably to one another before I came in and interrupted their conversation. They were all staring at me.

One of the babies tilted its head and spoke. She was a girl. "You must be Howie Quackenbush," she said.

"I am," I answered. "Who are you?"

"I'm your sister," she told me.

Chapter 18

The Hall of Babies was no larger than my living room. It was mostly empty, just the chairs and the babies and the net of umbilical cords. The ceiling was a sheet of transparent glass that looked into the water of the reservoir. I could see green plants waving slowly back and forth at the edges. The fish that swam past were gleaming in the light that shone up from the room. After I had been there for a few seconds, the babies began to relax and talk to one another again. The sight of so many babies chatting together was weird, and it made me feel a little bit jittery. I looked around for a place to sit down.

The baby who claimed to be my sister said, "If you want a chair, you can take Herbert's in just a second. He's about to be born—right, Herbert?"

The baby sitting next to her said, "That's right. It's

almost time now. Shouldn't be longer than—" Before he could finish, his umbilical cord gave a yank and he was sucked through the small hole in the wall. He disappeared with a sound like a cork popping out of a bottle. I was shocked. I guess that's what happens when babies are born.

"Please," said the first baby. "Have a seat."

Her arm sort of flipped toward the empty chair, and I sat down. She was looking at me, and I didn't know what to say to her. "Listen," I finally said, "you can't possibly be my sister. My sister hasn't even been born yet."

The baby said, "Do I look like *I've* been born yet?"

She had a point. Her eyes were a milky blue color, and she had a lot of wrinkles, more wrinkles than most babies do. Her head was almost completely bald, and what little hair she did have was plastered to her skull. Also, every once in a while she would turn in some random direction and flail her arms and legs. All the babies did that.

"But if you're my little sister, shouldn't you be inside my mom?" I asked. "What are you doing here?"

"I *am* inside your mom, but I'm also in the Hall of Babies," she said. "Haven't you ever been in two places at once?"

"Of course not," I said. "Nobody can be in two places at—" I stopped myself. I *had* been in two places at once. Just a few weeks ago, I had been in both my house and Casey Robinson's house at the same time. I remembered seeing her yellow bird Judy in the middle of my dad's bookshelf, her bathroom in the middle of my staircase, and her front hall floating in my backyard. I remembered holding on to her hand, and the way we seemed to drift through everything around us like it was made out of water. "Well . . . I guess I have been in two places at once."

"See," the baby said. "It's not that unusual. Lots of people have done it." She shifted in her armchair. "Most of us here have been in two places at once for five or six months now. Almost nine months in my case. In fact, now that Herbert's gone, I've been here longer than anybody else. I'm in a position of authority. People like me have to show the new guys the ropes, no pun intended." She tugged on her umbilical cord. "Anyway, Howie, I'm your sister, and I'm pleased to meet you. My name is Marie."

"No, it isn't," I said. I knew better: Mom and Dad had whittled *3,500 Names for Baby* down to about twenty names, but they hadn't chosen one yet. "You don't have a name yet. My mom and dad . . . *our* mom and dad"—I had decided that she was indeed my sister—"have been trying to decide what to name you for months now."

"I'm not going to argue with you," she said. "My name is Marie. You just know these things when you're down here. They might choose the *wrong* name, Mom and Dad— that happens more often than it should—but my real name will always be Marie."

"But that doesn't make any sense," I said. "Isn't your name whatever people call you?"

"Of course it is," Marie said, "but what people call you might not be your *true* name. And your true name is always the most important. You should have figured that out by now." Her hand twitched, and she accidentally poked herself in the face. "People will call you all sorts of things. Take Mom and Dad, for instance. You call them Mom and Dad, but their friends call them Lewis and Sylvia, and they call each other Honey sometimes, or Darling. I know. I've been listening."

"Well, you're right about that," I said. "So which one is their true name?"

"I don't know," Marie said. "You would have to ask them that, and they might not even know themselves. People tend to forget their true names after a while—that is, if it's not the name they're given at birth. In fact, if you're a person, rather than a building or a place, there's almost no way to discover your true name once you've forgotten it. That's why it's so important that parents choose the right name for their baby to begin with. Otherwise, how will you know who you are?"

"What about me?" I asked. "My name is Howie. Is that my true name or is it just what people call me?"

Marie shrugged her shoulders. Actually, she didn't exactly shrug her shoulders—she didn't have the muscle control for that. But she gave a little fidget, and I knew what she meant. "I know *my* true name, I don't know yours. But ask yourself if you feel like a Howie Quackenbush, and listen to what you have to say. That's the quickest way to find out."

I didn't know whether or not I felt like a Howie Quackenbush. I tried to think about it, but a turtle was crawling by on the ceiling, and I was sort of distracted by it. It's not too often that you get to see something walking from directly underneath. I watched its legs pushing against the glass, and the flat segments of its belly sliding past. After a few seconds, it gave up walking and began to swim. Turtles swim much faster than they crawl, and it vanished quickly into the murk of the reservoir.

It was nearing dinnertime, and most of the babies were talking to one another about the food they wanted to eat. "Is it almost time? I think it's almost time," they said, and "Monday night is pasta night," and "I hope it's not the yellow stuff again. I don't like the yellow stuff." Their voices filled the room with a constant low murmur.

Marie asked me a question. "What's the name of the food with the beans and the white meat and the chunks of green fruit?" she said.

"Chicken and avocado burritos from Señor Taco?" I suggested.

"That's the stuff," she said. She burped, and a bubble of spit burst open on her lips. This is one thing that's good about babies: they can do gross things and nobody thinks anything of it. "When I'm born, that's all I'm going to eat: chicken and avocado burritos from Señor Taco. I can't get enough of them."

I didn't have the heart to tell her that she would basically be eating mashed peas for the next twelve months. But there was something I did need to tell her. "Marie," I said. "I don't think you're going to get your true name when you're born. I'm sorry about that, but

Mom and Dad have been leaning toward naming you either Molly or Parker."

"Don't let them," she said. She said it simply and easily, with total trust in me. I was surprised by how good that made me feel. For the first time, I felt a little bit like her older brother.

I had all sorts of questions I wanted to ask her. I wondered, for instance, what happens to twins in the Hall of Babies: I pictured two babies crammed into one armchair, and two umbilical cords coming out of a single hole in the wall. I also wondered where Marie had been *before* she was in the Hall of Babies—whether she even knew. But it was almost five o'clock, and I knew that I had to leave soon if I wanted to get home before my parents began asking each other where I was. I got up from the armchair. "Well," I said, "I'd better be going now, Marie." I touched her hand: it was the softest thing I've ever felt in my life.

"Good-bye, Howie," she said. "I guess I'll see you soon."

I headed toward the wide yellow door, but I stopped before I got there. "*How* soon?" I asked Marie.

She made the little fidget that meant she was shrugging her shoulders again. "Soon," she said.

"Okay," I said. "Bye."

I opened the door, said "Multiparity," and transported back to my Aunt Margie's house. Before I left for home, I lit a stick of spicy vanilla incense, placed it in the incense holder, and left it smoking on the floor of the White Room.

I had gotten stuck with Larry Boone a few days before and had never made it back to the house, so I hadn't been able to light a stick that day even though I had promised I would. I felt bad about that. The White Room smelled as clean as it always did—no rotten egg smell—but still, I didn't want Aunt Margie to think that I had forgotten our agreement. I left a note telling her that I had been there, and I transported home.

Chapter 19

The next day, the workers with the orange hard hats were gone from the statue of Larry Boone. The wooden trestles with the DO NOT CROSS streamers had been cleared away, and the ground around the base of the statue had been filled in. Casey Robinson and I walked over to look at it. The soil had been laid down in baking pan–sized squares with green grass bristling from the tops. The grass all around it was still dead from the winter frost, so the block of green grass around the statue made it look like it was the only living thing in the whole schoolyard. I was pretty sure that the portal still worked. I figured that Larry Boone would have told us if it didn't. "It feels strange to be walking around up here when we know that Larry Boone is living right beneath us," Casey Robinson said.

"My mom is going to have a girl," I answered.

"What?!" Casey's face lit up, her cheeks red from the cold. "Your mom had her baby?"

"Not yet," I told her. "But it's going to be a girl when she does."

"How would you know that?"

"I met her," I said, and I told Casey Robinson about the Hall of Babies. I didn't want to keep it a secret, but I had to kind of stutter my way through the story. The problem was that I couldn't look at Casey without thinking about the fact that she had kissed me, and so I kept losing my train of thought. Midway through the story, the morning bell rang and the two of us had to rush inside. I told her that I would finish telling her all about the Hall of Babies later.

Kevin Bugg brought a big metal Crock-Pot to school that day, and we all wondered what he was doing with it. Miss Hufnagel placed it on a table in the corner of the room, and all morning it sat there making me curious. When I asked Kevin Bugg about it, he just smiled mysteriously and said, "You'll find out." About half an hour before lunch, Miss Hufnagel plugged the Crock-Pot in, and it began to heat up and bubble. The most wonderful smell drifted over the room. It turned out that Kevin Bugg had been practicing with the recipes in his *Great Onion Recipes for the Beginning Cook* book. He had made a lentil and onion stew the night before, and he'd brought enough to school for everyone to have a bowl with their lunch. The stew was really good! I was impressed, and I told Kevin Bugg so. He thanked me, and as we finished our lunch, he said, "I think I want to be a chef when I grow up. I've decided that it's what I want to do."

"Good for you," I told him, and I meant it. The stew was fantastic.

It was just before afternoon recess when the school secretary came to our door and whispered something into Miss Hufnagel's ear. Miss Hufnagel nodded and turned to the class. "Howie Quackenbush," she announced, "gather your things. Your aunt is waiting for you out front in her car."

The class was quiet and still for a second, and then everybody had questions to ask: "What's going on?" said Melissa McGee. "Is Howie in trouble?" said Casey Goss, the boy. "I bet it has something to do with the big smell," said Michael Jenkins. "Did they find the dead body?" said Nina Fitzsimmons.

Miss Hufnagel shook her head. "For the last time, Nina, there is no dead body—and no, Howie isn't in trouble. Howie is going to be a big brother." I got my backpack and my jacket and went outside. The class was still talking as I left.

My Aunt Margie was waiting for me in the curve of the front drive. "Hop in!" she said when she saw me coming down the stairway. "It's time!" Aunt Margie almost never drives her car. She prefers to walk or take the bus, and so she uses the car as a kind of rolling storage room. The backseat was covered with paint cans and carpenter's saws and blocks of dry-smelling wood. The front seat was filled with cotton balls in plastic bags, thousands of them.

These bags were in a big heap on the seat and the floor, and I had to burrow into them to make room for myself.

A nurse met us inside the hospital, the same nurse who had taken me to the waiting room on Sunday. She put her hand on my head and ruffled my hair. There's something about my hair that makes people want to ruffle it. I don't know why this should be, but it's true. The nurse looked at my Aunt Margie and said, "The delivery was a complete success. Your—sister?"

"Sister-in-law," said Aunt Margie.

"Your sister-in-law has had a healthy baby girl."

"Can we see them?" Aunt Margie asked.

The nurse nodded. "Of course. The baby is with them right now. I'll take you there myself if you'll give me just a second." She walked behind a counter and scribbled something down into a file folder, and then she drew a line through one of the names on the dry-erase marker board. "Okay," she said. "Follow me."

The hospital was busy with nurses and doctors and orderlies, but it was also strangely quiet. The sounds were few and far between, and I could hear them all very clearly: a bed wheeling past us, the beep of a heart monitor, two doctors talking in the hall. My mom and dad were sitting with the baby in a room with a big green curtain across the middle. Dad was wearing a pair of blue doctor's scrubs, and Mom was buried beneath a stack of white blankets. Her hair was hanging down the sides of her face in long, wet strands. They were both cooing over the baby. When they saw us come in, they broke into grins and called us over to the bed. "This is your little sister, Howie," my mom said. There were purple half moons beneath her eyes. "Would you like to hold her?"

I didn't know if I should. I was afraid I might not know how to hold her, that I would drop her or break her somehow. But my dad said, "Go ahead, Howie," so I took her in my arms.

She weighed almost nothing. She looked exactly like she had looked the day before, minus the umbilical cord and the armchair. I held her up to my shoulder and patted her on the back—I had seen people do this with babies before. I could my parents and Aunt Margie were surprised by how gentle I was being. I thought about how much fun it would be to take the baby transporting with me when she was a few years older, and I wondered if she would remember the Hall of Babies. Before I handed her back to my mom, I whispered something very softly into the baby's ear: "Remember me?" I asked, but she didn't say anything or look at me.

There was a knock on the door. "Mr. and Mrs. Quackenbush?" It was a man in a tie with a long white jacket. "It's time for us to finish filling out the birth certificate."

"Come on in, doctor," said my father.

The doctor pulled a chair over to the bed and began asking my mother questions. He needed to know her full maiden name and how it was spelled. He needed to know my father's full name and how *it* was spelled. (He didn't ask me for my name, which I have to say kind of disappointed me.) He needed to know what sex the baby was—or to confirm this, since he had been there for the delivery. He needed to know our place of residence, both town and street. "Okay," he said, crossing the *t* in North Mellwood. "The last thing I need from you is your baby's name."

"The moment of truth," said my Aunt Margie, giving a one-note laugh.

My mom and dad looked at each other, and I could see that they had not yet agreed on a name. I had heard them talking about it the night before. My mom still liked "Parker," and my dad was lobbying for either "Grace" or "Stinkweed." These were the wrong names, and I knew it.

"Marie," I said. "Her name is Marie."

Everybody turned to stare at me—my mom, my dad, Aunt Margie, the doctor. I felt like I had just dropped a tray of dishes or something. I began to blush.

But then, slowly, a look came over my parents' faces. First it seemed like they were remembering something. And then, after a second, it seemed like they were discovering something.

They smiled at each other. "Marie," my mom said to my dad. "Marie," my dad said to my mom. They leaned down over the baby, who was sound asleep on my mom's chest.

My dad kissed the baby on the ear. My mom ran a finger down her cheek. "Hello, baby," they said. "Hello, Marie."

Acknowledgments

I owe thanks to my editor Regina Hayes, senior editor Melanie Cecka, my agent Kyung Cho, the administrators of the James Michener-Paul Engle Fellowship for financial support, and Patricia Lawrence, Heather McDonough, and Koalani Colvin for early readings.